The Door-to-Door Deception

River Heights Park was about a dozen blocks away from the community center. The streets the kids and counselors had to cross were not busy, and the kids behaved themselves on the trip.

Once in the park, George led the group down a long sloping path that ended at a wide promenade overlooking the river that ran through the town and gave it its name.

As Nancy approached the riverbank, she looked back to make sure that no skaters were lagging behind. She lifted the front of her right skate off the pavement, hoping to engage the heel brake so she could slow down.

Suddenly Nancy felt a jolt, as if she had skated over a big bump. But the pavement was smooth. She looked down and gasped in horror.

The rubber brake pad had come off Nancy's skate. The pavement dipped sharply, and Nancy could do nothing to slow herself as she careened wildly toward the riverbank.

Nancy Drew
Mystery Stories

Available from MINSTREL Books

NANCY DREW® 140

THE DOOR-TO-DOOR DECEPTION

CAROLYN KEENE

A MINSTREL® BOOK

Published by POCKET BOOKS
New York London Toronto Sydney Tokyo Singapore

A MINSTREL PAPERBACK *Original*

A Minstrel Book published by
POCKET BOOKS, a division of Simon & Schuster Inc.
1230 Avenue of the Americas, New York, NY 10020

Copyright © 1997 by Simon & Schuster Inc.
Produced by Mega-Books, Inc.

ISBN: 0-671-00053-5

First Minstrel Books printing December 1997

10 9 8 7 6 5 4 3 2 1

NANCY DREW, NANCY DREW MYSTERY STORIES, A MINSTREL BOOK and colophon are registered trademarks of Simon & Schuster Inc.

Cover art by Ernie Norcia

Printed in the U.S.A.

Contents

THE DOOR-TO-DOOR
DECEPTION

1

Helping Out

"I don't get it," Bess Marvin said as she looked at her watch. "George is never late. I wonder what's keeping her."

"She's been so busy recently," Nancy Drew said. "When she's working with the kids at that community center, she loses all track of time. Her job sounds intense, but she really loves it."

Bess gave Nancy a sideways glance, then grinned. "Has George been after you to do some volunteering, too?" she asked. "Every time I talk to her, it's always, 'So, when are you going to come see the place?'"

"Okay, I give up. When?" a familiar voice demanded.

Nancy glanced over her shoulder and gave

George Fayne a welcoming smile. At five feet eight, George was taller than both Nancy and Bess. Her short, brown hair formed a curly cap on her head. She was wearing her usual outfit—faded jeans, a T-shirt, and running shoes.

"I'm sorry I'm late, you guys," George said, out of breath. "A couple of kids got into an argument and I didn't want to leave until things were straightened out."

"No problem," Nancy said. "We're next in line for a table, so your timing is perfect."

"A little too perfect," Bess added with a grin. "If I didn't know you better, I'd say you planned it this way."

The three friends were meeting for lunch after their various morning activities. They had picked the mall as a place to meet because it was centrally located. Now they were led to an empty table next to the railing, overlooking a fountain on the main plaza level.

"It's good to sit down," Bess said as she sank into her seat and rested shopping bags against her chair. She glanced at the menu. "I'll have a burger and an iced tea," she said when the waitress appeared.

George ordered a turkey burger and Nancy ordered an avocado and sprouts sandwich on pita bread.

"You guys are too healthy for me," Bess said. "Give me a good old hamburger any day."

"Speaking of healthy," George said, "have you thought about an afternoon or two volunteering at CARING? It's rewarding, it's good exercise, and it helps a lot of kids."

"I'm thinking about it," Nancy replied. "What does the name stand for again?"

"Community After-school Recreation In Neighborhood Groups," George said. "It's a really great program. We have sports, crafts, discussion groups, and creative writing. The kids are mostly junior-high-school age, and the counselors are really terrific. Next Saturday, we're having an in-line skating marathon. If you were to start now, you could be part of it."

"I'd like to find out more about the program," Nancy replied. "But I'm not sure I'd have much time to devote to it right now."

"Whatever time you could give would be a help," George said. "Bess? How about you?"

"I don't know. You know I'm not much of an athlete, George," Bess replied.

"I'm not expecting you to coach the field hockey team," George said. "There's a lot more to CARING than sports. One of our big efforts now is raising money for the program by selling cartons of high-energy snack bars door-to-door. You'd be terrific at that."

"High-energy snack bars?" Bess repeated. She glanced down at the bean sprouts on Nancy's plate. "You know how I feel about health food, George."

"You don't have to eat them," George replied quickly. "Just sell tons of them. I have an idea. How about if I take you both over to the recreation center tomorrow afternoon, show you around, and introduce you to the director, Lena Boling. She's been with the organization for about a year, and from what everybody says, she's made a real difference in that time. I think you'll see why CARING's so important to me."

"Fair enough," Nancy said. Bess nodded her agreement.

The next afternoon, Nancy picked up George and Bess in her blue Mustang. It was a beautiful day—sunny and not too chilly.

"Which way, George?" Nancy asked as she backed out of the Fayne driveway.

"It's on the South Side, across the street from Washington Park," George told her.

"I know where that is," Nancy said. "It's near one of my favorite antique stores."

Twenty minutes later, Nancy turned onto Washington Avenue. Old trolley tracks were visible down the center of the asphalt. Brick build-

4

ings from the turn of the century lined both sides of the street.

"Turn left at the next corner," George said.

Nancy turned the car onto a tree-shaded street and drove by a row of modest, neatly kept homes. The houses were nearly touching, but each one had a small patch of lawn out front. There were basketball hoops mounted on many of the garages and bicycles leaned on kickstands in the driveways.

Two blocks later, a large park appeared on the right.

"This is pretty," Bess said.

"It's called Washington Park," George said. "You'll love it. It's got everything—a municipal pool, tennis courts, playing fields, even a nature trail. And CARING is over there," she added, pointing to a redbrick building on the corner. "We can park around the side."

Nancy drove around the corner of the building and pulled into a parking spot. As they got out of the car, she glanced up at the building. It was three stories high, with a gray slate roof and four brick chimneys, one of which was clearly in disrepair. To Nancy, the place looked as if it had seen better days. A sign on the lawn read Clelland Recreation Center. A smaller wooden sign below it read C.A.R.I.N.G.

"The Clelland family built this house and lived

here for many years," George explained as they started up the walk. "They left it to the town. CARING shares it with other community organizations."

Nancy paused to admire the panels of stained glass on either side of the oak front door. Then she followed George and Bess inside.

They found themselves standing in a huge entrance hall. On the left was a large rectangular room with an elaborate fireplace at the far end. Nancy could see French doors, which led to a glassed-in porch.

They climbed the wide stairs to the second floor. One of the doors down the hall was open. George tapped on it, then went in.

"Hi, Lena," she said. "I'd like you to meet my friends Bess Marvin and Nancy Drew. They're thinking about doing some work here."

"Oh, yes. Come on in," Lena replied.

Lena's round face, pert nose, and pixie-cut black hair made her look about twelve years old. But Nancy figured that Lena had to be at least in her twenties.

"What do you say we start with a quick overview?" Lena said. She led them to some folding chairs near the windows.

As soon as they were all seated, Lena began. "What's different about CARING is that it's aimed at kids in their early teens. There are lots

6

of programs for grade-school kids. And by high school, there's not as much need for a structured program. But in between, there's a real need for a program like this. A lot of our children come from single-parent families or families where both parents work. That means no one's home when they get out of school. We're trying to fill that gap by offering an exciting after-school program."

"How big is the program?" Bess asked.

"We have around sixty-five kids signed up now," Lena said. "Not all of them come every day, though. Our goal is to be about twice that size. What's holding us back is lack of money and a shortage of counselors. We depend entirely on volunteers. We simply don't have money for paid staff." With a laugh, she added, "We can't even afford the tiny salaries the treasurer and I earn—when we get them, that is."

"You'd really enjoy working here," George told Nancy. "I know you would. And you'd make a terrific counselor."

"Have you had any experience working with children?" Lena asked. "Do you have any special skills? Sports? Crafts?"

"Nancy is good at just about every sport. And Bess has done tons of baby-sitting," George said quickly. "I know they'll be great with the kids."

Lena turned to gaze out the window. After a

moment, she said, "Why don't you try it out this week? We could work out a flexible schedule. No commitments on either side. It would be like a trial period."

Nancy glanced at Bess, who gave a hesitant nod. "Okay. I'll give it a shot," Bess said.

"I will, too," Nancy said.

"All *right*," George said.

"Good. I know you'll find it rewarding," Lena said. She stood up. "Would you like to take a look around?"

"Sure," Nancy said.

Lena walked to the door. "Josh?" she called. "Do you have a minute?"

A moment later, a young man appeared in the doorway. He gave Nancy, Bess, and George a warm smile. He was tall, with broad shoulders and sandy-colored hair.

Nancy returned Josh's smile. Then she caught a glimpse of the dreamy expression on Bess's face. Nancy smiled to herself. Bess clearly found Josh attractive.

"Josh, I want you and George to give Bess and Nancy a quick tour."

"No problem," Josh said. "We can start with the girls' soccer game."

"Great," Bess said. "I love soccer."

Nancy caught George's eye and the two smiled.

"This should be a lively game," Josh said as he held the front door. "We're playing the YES team."

"YES is another youth program," George explained. "The two teams share the facilities of the park and they're traditional rivals."

"Good-natured rivals, I hope," Nancy said. "That could make things pretty exciting."

From the other side of a band of trees came a burst of cheers and groans. Josh started walking faster. The three girls hurried after him.

Soon they reached the soccer field. Josh went over to speak to one of the spectators, then rejoined the girls. "YES just scored, so we're down, one-zip," he said. "It could be worse, I guess. We're the team in the green shirts."

Nancy scanned the field. The CARING goal was close enough for her to see the look of determination on the goalkeeper's face. The look turned to frustration, Nancy noticed. She looked down the field and saw the YES center forward ahead of the pack, kicking the ball up the field with no opposition.

The goalie shifted to the left, anticipating the shot, hoping to block it. The YES forward spotted the movement and quickly passed to a teammate.

Nancy held her breath as she watched the scene unfold. The goal was wide open, she knew.

An instant later, a burst of cheers came from the YES supporters as the ball found its mark and a point was scored.

"Too bad," Nancy said to her companions. She saw that George had been watching the action, too, but Bess was deep in conversation with Josh.

The dejected CARING goalie picked up the ball and tossed it in the direction of the referee. It fell short, landing at the feet of another CARING player, a girl with long dark hair.

Her face set in anger, the dark-haired girl gave the ball a hard sideways kick. It came cannoning toward the sideline—right where Bess and Josh were standing.

2

Foul Play

"Watch out!" George shouted. Pushing past Nancy, she lunged in front of Bess and Josh, then leaped into the air and hit the ball solidly with her head. The ball soared high and practically dropped into the arms of the astonished referee.

"George, are you all right?" Nancy cried out.

"I'm fine," George replied with a grin. "That's a basic soccer maneuver. Pretty cool, isn't it?"

"I'll say," Josh said. "You saved me and Bess from being badly bruised."

"Thank you, thank you," George said as she pretended to bow to the crowd. Then she turned to Nancy, Bess, and Josh and added a bit sheepishly, "I know I could have just caught the ball and tossed it back. But this way was more fun. I guess I'm just a ham at heart."

The CARING coach appeared at the sideline and called to the dark-haired girl. "Brittany, come over here. We need to talk."

The dark-haired girl walked off the field. Her feet dragged and her face was sullen. The coach spoke to her quietly. Then she took the girl's elbow and steered her over to the spot where George, Bess, and Nancy were standing.

"Brittany has something to say to you," the coach told them. "Don't you, Brittany?"

Brittany stared down at her soccer shoes. Close-up, she looked younger than Nancy had thought, barely twelve.

"Yeah. I'm sorry I lost my temper and kicked the ball so hard," she said in a low voice. "I wasn't trying to hit any of you. Honest."

"Thanks for the apology, Brittany," George said warmly. "You know, when you get mad at the ball, you're pretty powerful. You should kick like that during the game."

Brittany glanced at George, then shrugged and looked at the ground. Then she looked at the coach, as if asking permission to leave. The coach nodded and patted her shoulder, and Brittany went back out to the field.

"Sorry about that," the coach said, once Brittany was out of hearing range. "I'm Kiara Baum," she added, smiling at Bess and Nancy.

Nancy and Bess introduced themselves. "I'm giving them a tour," George said. "They've decided to take a shot at being counselors."

"If they don't get beaned by a soccer ball first," Josh said. He shook his head. "Kiara, what's with Brittany, losing her cool like that?"

"She's been having some problems lately," Kiara said. "I'd better get back to my game. I'll look for you guys afterward. Maybe I can help correct your first impression of this place."

Kiara walked back to the tight cluster of players watching from the field. At the next time-out, she sent several girls in to replace players who were in the game.

One of the players replaced was Brittany. Nancy saw her trying to hide a scowl as she came off the field.

The presence of the new players seemed to motivate the rest of the team. When the other team's pass went out of bounds, the CARING player kicked it neatly over her opponents' heads to a waiting teammate. Before the YES players could mount a defense, the ball was sailing into the goal.

"Good going!" Josh exclaimed, as the cheers died down. "Finally."

13

"This is a pretty intense game," Bess remarked. "Why is everyone so competitive?"

"That's what sports are all about," George said. "Competition—and winning."

"Also, sports are a good outlet for the anger that many kids feel about the situations they're in. It's a great way to blow off steam. Besides," he added with a smile, "we're playing YES, and the rivalry is fierce. Would you mind if we stuck around to see the end of the game?"

"Fine with me," Bess said, moving a step closer to Josh. "This is very exciting."

Nothing like a handsome young man to spark Bess's interest in sports, Nancy thought.

Nancy and George sat in the stands on the sidelines. They could see that both teams were putting all they had into the game. The players were as determined to defend their goal as they were to score. In spite of many attempts at goals from both sides, the score stayed frozen at two-one in favor of YES.

During the next time-out, a young woman with shoulder-length black hair walked past. "Hey, Maria," George called out. "Do you have a minute? I'd like you to meet my friends, Nancy and Bess. I told you about them the other day."

Maria walked over. The color in her cheeks made her look excited, but the expression in her dark eyes was cool, even reserved, Nancy noticed.

"I remember," she said, nodding to Bess, who had joined them, and to Nancy. "You were hoping to get them into the program."

"I think I succeeded, too," George said. Nancy noticed she was purposefully ignoring Maria's distant attitude. "They're going to give it a try this week. Isn't that great?"

"That's very generous of you," Maria said, looking from Nancy to Bess. "I know you'll find this work quite rewarding."

"I'm sure we will," Nancy replied, trying to sound warm.

"Well, nice to meet you," Maria said. "Excuse me—I have some work to take care of."

As Maria walked away, Bess said, "Brrr! What was that about?"

"I'm not sure," George said. "Maria grew up a few blocks from here. She was in CARING when she was a kid. The program was a lot smaller then. That was before Lena came in and began to expand the program. Maybe Maria wishes it were still the way it used to be."

"Or maybe to her, we're outsiders because we live on the other side of town," Nancy said. "I could understand her feeling that way. I just hope she gives us a chance."

"Well," Bess said, "whatever the reason, she didn't exactly go out of her way to make us feel welcome."

Josh stood a few feet in front of them, closer to the field. His back had been to them as he followed the play. Now he walked back to the stands.

"Don't worry about Maria," he said. "The rest of us will make sure you feel welcome. Right, George?"

"You bet," George said, keeping her eyes on the field. The game was on again and George started cheering, "Go, Pam! Go!"

A tall, thin girl with a red ponytail was charging down the field with the ball. One of the YES players moved to intercept, but she faked right, then dodged past her to the left.

"Go for it, Pam! Kick the ball!" George shouted.

Pam drove straight for the goal, her red hair flying behind her. The YES goalie was already in place to block the attempt. Could Pam get the ball past her? Nancy leaned forward in anticipation.

At the last possible moment, Pam made a rapid pass to her left. Another CARING player was there to receive it. Perfectly in line to score, she kicked the ball hard into the net. The CARING spectators roared their approval.

The girl who had scored the goal gave a high five and a broad smile to Pam. It took Nancy a few moments to realize that the player who had scored the goal was Brittany. She looked like a different person when she smiled, Nancy thought.

Over the cheers, George exclaimed, "Wasn't that great!"

"It sure was," Josh said. "It's about time we started showing these guys what we can do."

A tall young man with blond hair, who had been standing a few feet away, suddenly walked over. "We're ahead three games to one this season, and today will make four. Face it, Josh, you're toast."

"No way, Kyle," Josh replied. "This game is far from over."

Kyle smirked. "Your team doesn't have a chance," he said. "You'll see." He turned and strode away.

Josh looked around and shrugged. "These games tend to have a strange effect on people around here. He can actually be a nice guy."

"Does everybody take this rivalry so seriously?" Nancy asked.

"You could say that," Josh said.

"But why?" asked Bess. "It seems so childish."

"It goes way back, I guess," Josh said. "It used to be that kids on our side of the park went to one school, and the kids on the other side went to a rival school. The schools are consolidated now, but people around here still remember."

"There's something else, too," George said. "The facilities. When YES is using the tennis courts or the baseball diamond, for instance, we can't. So there's some tension."

"And then there's funding," Josh said. "Whether it's money from the city or from private donors, we're basically both competing for the same money. The more they get, the less there is for us, and vice versa. The situation's tailor-made for creating tension and hostility."

"Why doesn't somebody do something about it?" Bess asked. "Can't everyone see that they share the same goal?"

"I know," Josh told her. "Lena says we have more important problems to focus on and that we should concentrate on helping the kids. I know she's right."

"Go, go!" George suddenly yelled.

Nancy looked around. One of the CARING forwards was bringing the ball down the field. The YES goal looked wide-open. Then, as if from nowhere, a YES player ran in front of her and stole the ball.

Brittany was the nearest player to defend the goal. She ran toward the YES player and tried to take away the ball. Suddenly she was down, writhing on the ground, clutching her stomach. The YES player zipped around her and took a shot. It was good.

The referee gave four or five blasts on her whistle. The game was over.

Kiara ran over to Brittany, who was just getting to her feet. Nancy saw Brittany shake her head, as if to say, "I'm okay."

"We won! We won!" the YES cheering section chanted.

"Foul! Foul!" the CARING spectators chanted back.

"Did you see that?" Josh exclaimed. "It was an obvious foul. That goal shouldn't count!"

Nancy didn't know what to say. She hadn't actually seen what had happened. And, clearly, neither had the referee. According to the rules, Nancy knew, that meant the goal was good. YES was the winner.

A few feet away, two boys of about twelve began to call each other names and push each other. Nancy could tell they were working themselves up into a full-blown fight. She started toward them, sensing that Josh was right behind her.

Nancy pushed between the two boys and said, "Okay, guys, chill out. It's just a game."

The boy on her left refused to look at her, but he took half a step backward. Nancy felt encouraged. Then she saw his eyes widen in alarm. She looked around. The boy on her right was lunging toward Nancy with an expression of hatred on his face.

3

Door-to-Door Danger

For an instant, Nancy was stunned by the unexpected attack. Then her trained instincts took over. Turning sideways to present a smaller target, she leaned forward to divert the boy's lunge safely. Her shoulder caught his arm, supplying just enough push to throw him off balance. He took a stumbling step forward, then straightened up and looked around, confused.

"Dino, stop that! Get hold of yourself!" Josh rushed over and put an arm around the boy's shoulders. It looked like a friendly enough gesture, but Nancy could tell that Josh was definitely on guard.

"Let me go!" Dino demanded. "I'm going to get him!"

"You're going to take a deep breath, count to ten, and calm down," Josh said sternly. "You know the rule: no fighting."

"That kid said mean things about our group," Dino protested. "He called us names."

"That wasn't very nice of him," Josh said. "But why take it out on Nancy?"

"Who?" Dino blinked and seemed to notice Nancy for the first time.

"Dino, this is Nancy Drew," Josh said.

Nancy smiled and said, "Hi, Dino."

"Nancy's a good friend of George's," Josh continued. "I'm showing her and her friend Bess around. We're hoping that they'll decide to work as counselors. But what'll they think if our kids attack them?"

"Sorry," Dino said. He stared down at his foot as he traced a pattern in the dirt. "I didn't even see her, I was so mad. Besides, the other kid started it."

"It takes two to fight," Josh began.

"I know," Dino said. "But it's hard to remember when somebody's in your face, that's all."

"Of course it's hard," Josh said. "But that's when you need to remember it most. Okay?"

"Okay." Dino started to turn away. Then he looked back and met Nancy's gaze. "I'm sorry I almost knocked you down," he said.

"That's okay, Dino," Nancy said.

"Now, get moving," Josh said. "Snack time."

Dino grinned and jogged away to catch up to a group of kids who were walking back toward the rec center.

"I liked the way you handled that," Josh told Nancy. "Do you know martial arts? Maybe you could give a workshop for the kids. I know it'd be a big hit."

"I'm not a black belt or anything," Nancy said, "but I'd be happy to show some of the basics of self-defense." She noticed that Maria was standing a few feet away, obviously listening. Her expression was as cold as before.

"Come on," Josh said, looking around to include Maria along with Nancy, Bess, and George. "If we don't hurry, the kids will finish all the cookies and juice."

"I'll be along later," Maria said, and walked away.

Josh watched her go with an unhappy frown. Then he shrugged. "She'll get over it," he said.

Nancy wasn't so sure. Maria didn't seem to want to get over anything. She could really make things unpleasant for everyone, Nancy thought to herself.

On the walk back to the center, Bess stayed close to Josh. They were talking about the soccer game. George fell back to join Nancy.

"What do you think?" George asked.

"Well," Nancy began. "I can see why you're so involved in this group. The kids really need lots of love and attention. I think I can help with that. I'd like to give it a try."

"I'm glad," George replied. "The kids need you. I know things got off to a rocky start. But you'll have fun. I'm being selfish, too. I'd really like having you and Bess around."

"I'm in," Nancy said. "And I can see Bess is, too, though for different reasons."

"Maybe you and Bess can start by selling energy bars this afternoon," George continued. "I'd go with you, but right after snack time I'm scheduled to lead a Ping-Pong clinic."

"I didn't know you were a Ping-Pong expert," Nancy said, giving her a quizzical look.

"I'm not," she confessed. "But I play better than the kids do."

"One thing, though," Nancy said with a laugh. "If you use that referee, you'd better buy her some glasses."

When they reached the rec center, Josh led them down the back stairs to the basement rec room. Dozens of kids were milling around, talking and laughing.

Nancy, Bess, and George edged through the crowd to the refreshment table. Only a few crumbs were left on the cookie plates, but they managed to get four cups of apple cider.

Someone tapped Nancy on the arm and said, "Hi." It was Dino.

"Hi, there," Nancy said.

"Are you really going to be a counselor?" Dino asked. "Would you show me how you blocked me before? It was cool."

"Absolutely," Nancy replied. "It's a martial arts move. It's not about fighting, it's about *not* fighting."

"If you'll teach me, I'd like to learn," Dino said.

"Sounds good," Nancy said.

George had disappeared into the crowd. Now she returned with Lena.

"Lena agrees it's a good idea for you and Bess to make the rounds with the energy bars."

"Usually, we send out teams, a couple of counselors together with two or three of the kids," Lena said. "People seem to buy more from kids. But all the kids who signed up to sell this afternoon are already out, and every little bit helps. Let's go up to my office and I'll fill you in on what you need to know."

"This neighborhood looks like it can afford to buy plenty of energy bars," Bess said.

Nancy stopped the Mustang at the curb and looked around. Bess was right. The houses here were big and new, with two-car garages and large, well-kept lawns.

Bess giggled. "Maybe they need more energy so they can afford to pay for their houses." She looked around, her smile beginning to fade. "The truth is, I feel bad ringing doorbells so close to dinnertime."

"Me, too," Nancy admitted. "But Lena's right. That's when you catch people at home. Come on, I think we're stalling. How about you take this side of the street, and I'll take the other, all the way down to the end. We can meet back at the car when we're done. Then I'll drop you at home."

"What about George?" Bess asked. "Isn't she expecting a ride?"

Nancy shook her head. "No, she told me she'd get a lift from one of the other counselors."

Nancy grabbed her sales kit from the backseat, straightened her green CARING T-shirt, and walked briskly across the street. The street sign at the corner read Markham Lane.

She stopped at the first house and pressed the doorbell. At first there was silence and then a burst of angry barking came from inside. Claws scratched loudly on the inside of the door.

Nancy waited. The barking and scratching continued, but she didn't hear any noises that sounded as if someone were home. "Oh, well," she murmured after a minute.

She returned to the street and went on to the next house. A young woman answered the door. She explained that she was the nanny and that Ms. Flynn wouldn't be home for another hour.

The people at the next two houses politely refused to buy. At the third, the woman slammed the door before Nancy even finished saying why she was there.

By the time she reached the end of the second block, Nancy was beginning to feel discouraged. She rang the bell of the corner house and was surprised when the door opened and a pleasant-looking man looked at her with curiosity. "Yes?" he asked.

Nancy told him about CARING and gave him a brochure. He glanced at it while she explained that they were taking orders for high-energy snack bars.

"Do they taste good?" he asked.

Nancy felt her face start to redden. "Uh, I don't really know," she said. "This is my first day with the program. I haven't tried one yet."

The man smiled. "An honest salesperson— how refreshing! All right, young lady. Put me down for one carton. And if they *don't* taste good, that's all right, too. I know the money is going to a good cause."

Nancy filled out the order sheet exactly the way that Lena had instructed, gave the man his copy, and thanked him. As she walked to the next house, she thought what a difference one nice person could make. The task of selling energy bars seemed so much more possible now.

At the first house on the next block, no one answered the door. Nancy turned to go back to the street. A curtain moved in one of the front windows. Someone *was* there, peeking out. Nancy was sure of it. She shrugged and continued down the street.

At the next house, a middle-aged woman came to the door. She listened as Nancy started her sales pitch. Then she held up her hand.

"Don't waste your breath," she said. "We had one of your people here just last week. I told her I didn't want any. I still don't."

"Sorry to bother you," Nancy said. Back at the street, she paused. Had someone else from CARING really been there already? Or had the woman said that simply as a way of getting rid of her? She looked at the house number—304. Then she checked the piece of paper Lena had given her. It read "Nos. 100–200 on Markham." They didn't match.

She looked around, then realized what must have happened. Lena had assigned her only the first two blocks on this street. Someone else must have covered this third block the week before.

Nancy returned to the corner and started across the street. A block farther down, a police car rounded the corner onto Markham. Suddenly its lights started flashing. The engine roared as it accelerated in her direction. Nancy stepped back up onto the curb to let it pass.

Brakes screeched as the patrol car swerved to the curb and stopped just a few feet from her. Startled, Nancy backed away. The front doors banged open, and the two officers jumped out with their guns drawn.

"Freeze!" one of them shouted at Nancy. "Don't move a muscle!"

4

Trouble Down the Block

"Drop the bag! Both hands on the roof of the car," one of the police officers ordered.

Nancy let the CARING sales kit fall to the ground and leaned against the police car. The second officer, a woman, patted her down.

"Okay, straighten up, nice and slow, and turn around," the female officer said. She took a step back.

Nancy did as she was told.

"Let's see some ID," the male officer said. His name tag read Velez. "What's your business here?" he asked Nancy.

Nancy showed him her driver's license and said, "I'm a volunteer with a community organization called CARING. We're selling high-energy snack bars door-to-door. What's the matter, Officer Velez?"

He looked at her license, then passed it to his partner. Nancy noticed her name tag read Mahone. Officer Mahone glanced at the license quickly and was about to hand it back when she looked down once more.

"Nancy Drew," she said. "Is your father a lawyer?"

"That's right," Nancy said. She couldn't tell from the officer's tone if this fact was in her favor or not.

"I guess you're not connected with a burglary ring, then, are you?" Mahone continued.

"Burglary ring?" Nancy repeated. "No!"

"There've been some break-ins around here in the last couple of weeks," Velez said. "That house on the corner was one of the targets. So when the fellow who lives there heard his doorbell ring and saw a stranger on his front porch, he called us to report a suspicious prowler. We came right over."

"A suspicious prowler? Me?" Nancy said. "But all I did was walk up to the front door and ring the bell."

"When people hear there's been a burglary on their block, it makes them jumpy," Mahone explained.

31

"Let me give you some advice," Velez said. "You and your organization have a perfect right to solicit door-to-door. But you'd be smart to let us know what neighborhoods you're planning to cover. It's for your own protection."

"I'll be sure to pass that along to the person in charge," Nancy said. "To tell you the truth, this is my first time out."

"Is that right?" Mahone said. "Are those snack bars any good?"

Nancy blushed. "I haven't had time to try one yet," she confessed.

The radio in the patrol car crackled. Velez listened for a moment, then said, "We've got to get going, Ms. Drew. Sorry we had to stop you. But remember what I said, and be sure to pass it along."

"I will," Nancy promised.

The two officers got back in their car and drove away. Nancy watched thoughtfully. Then she picked up her sales kit and walked back to her car to wait for Bess.

"Wow!" Bess said, after Nancy told her about the encounter with the police. "The only thing that happened to me was that a terrier tried to bite my ankle. But it was just a puppy. And the owner ordered two cartons of energy bars—one cocoa and one banana. I think he felt guilty."

Being a lawyer's daughter, Nancy had a different idea about why the dog's owner might have wanted to buy Bess's goodwill. "He was probably afraid you'd sue him," she said with a smile.

That evening, during dinner, Nancy told her father about becoming a volunteer for CARING.

"CARING? I've heard good things about the organization," Mr. Drew said. "One of my clients is on the board. He approached me for a contribution last year."

"The kids I'd be working with can really use some help," Nancy said. "And I don't even mind selling energy bars door-to-door. What I didn't much like was being treated the way I was by the police."

"What's this?" her father said, in mock alarm. "Police harassment?"

Nancy explained what had happened.

Mr. Drew stroked his chin thoughtfully. "Well, I don't think you should blame the police for being a little off the mark. They have reason to be on edge. But you're right. Being told to freeze by two officers with drawn guns is not a pleasant experience."

Nancy nodded. "They said something about burglaries. . . ."

"Yes. It hasn't hit the papers yet, but there have been a number of burglaries of homes in that area lately," her father said.

"Is it a burglary ring?" Nancy asked.

"From what I hear, the police aren't sure," Mr. Drew replied. "Burglary rings usually specialize in a particular neighborhood. But these have been all over town. Still, there are some common features. For one thing, all the robberies have taken place during the day. For another, the burglars seem to know when the houses will be empty and how to get around the alarm systems."

"Do the police have any leads?" Nancy asked.

Carson Drew smiled. "They don't always share their secrets with me," he said. "I hear things now and then, that's all."

"Wouldn't it be cool if I could break the case for them!" Nancy said. Nancy was well known as a detective, even outside of River Heights. She had solved tricky cases all over the country.

"Don't get carried away," Mr. Drew said. "This string of burglaries is the sort of crime that's best handled by the police. They're trained and equipped for the kind of work that will solve it. But tell me more about these energy bars. How do they taste?"

"Everyone keeps asking me that," Nancy said. "I'll try one tonight for dessert."

"Aha, caught you," her father joked, pointing an accusing finger at her. "Flagrant misrepresentation. That's an obvious tort!"

"It's not a *torte*, Dad, it's a snack bar," Nancy quipped. "I just haven't had time to try one yet."

"Never mind," Mr. Drew said, smiling. "Did you sell any?"

"Bess did a little better than I did," Nancy said. "But we both got some orders."

"Great. And as for the police, that was good advice they gave you. I'd feel better about your ringing strangers' doorbells if I knew that the authorities were aware of where you were and what you were doing."

"Okay, Dad," Nancy said. She had to admit that she also had uneasy feelings about going up to the homes of strangers. "I promise—from now on, we submit a flight plan before takeoff."

The next afternoon, Nancy pulled up outside Bess's house and gave a quick tap on her horn. After a pause, Bess came running out the door, holding half a sandwich.

Bess climbed in. "No George?" she asked as she fastened her seat belt.

"She called to say she was going earlier," Nancy replied as they drove away.

Bess held out her sandwich. "I'm running so

late, I didn't have time to finish lunch. Want a bite? Peanut butter and banana."

Nancy laughed. "Sounds like a great flavor for an energy bar. Have you tried them yet? They're pretty good."

Bess nodded. "Although they tasted a little *too* healthy, if you know what I mean. Are we selling again today?"

"I have no idea," Nancy said, shaking her head. "If we do, I hope we go with some of the kids. It'd be more fun that way. The whole idea is to have a lot of contact with them."

"Like the contact you almost had with that kid Dino yesterday?" Bess teased.

"That was just a misunderstanding," Nancy said. "Dino turned out to be a nice kid."

"That must be why he goes around shoving people," Bess said. She leaned forward to turn on the car radio.

When they reached the center, Nancy parked her car and the two girls went inside. Upstairs, the door to Lena's office was partly open. Nancy tapped, then looked inside. The room was empty.

"We might as well wait in here," she said. "Lena's bound to be back in a couple of minutes."

On the wall behind Lena's desk, Nancy noticed a large street map of River Heights. Small areas in different sections of town had been outlined, then crossed off with a red marker.

"Look," Nancy said. "I'll bet those are the blocks that people have already covered in the sales campaign." She went over to the map and located the neighborhood she and Bess had been to the previous afternoon. The blocks she'd been on were marked. But not the one she'd gone to by mistake.

"That's funny," Nancy said. "Yesterday a woman told me that somebody had already been to her house last week selling energy bars. But her block isn't marked on this map."

"Maybe Lena's fallen behind in marking the map," Bess suggested. "Or maybe the woman simply wanted to get rid of you without hurting your feelings."

"That's probably it," Nancy agreed with a laugh. "What she didn't realize is that when you're selling door-to-door, you try not to *have* feelings."

The office door swung open. "Oh, hi," Lena said as she walked in. "It's great to see you both. Did you meet our treasurer, Alex Houston?"

Just behind her was a man in his early twenties, with short brown hair and brown eyes. He was of medium height, a couple of inches taller than Nancy, and muscular. He was wearing a light blue T-shirt and tight, faded jeans.

"Hey, there," Alex said. He gave them a casual wave. As he did, the side of the shopping bag he was carrying split, spilling out dozens of CDs onto the floor.

Nancy and Bess knelt to help Alex retrieve the CDs. Nancy noticed that they were all new jazz recordings, still wrapped in plastic. He must have just come from the record store, she figured.

"Are you a collector?" she asked as she passed him some of the CDs.

"I'm just getting started," he replied. "But there's so much out there, it's crazy. Today I saw a boxed set of one of my favorite jazz musicians. Twelve CDs, all from just one series of recording sessions. One hundred sixty bucks. I hated to leave it behind."

Bess gasped. Nancy was less astonished. She had just found Alex's cash register receipt where it had fallen under the desk. This particular batch of CDs had cost him $318 and change. She passed him the receipt. He crumpled it up and stuck it in his back pocket.

"So, how was the selling yesterday?" Lena asked, when they finished picking up the CDs.

"All right," Nancy said. She related her encounter with the police and the Officer Velez's parting advice.

Lena tugged at her lower lip. When Nancy finished, she said, "I thought about telling the police our plans. But I figured they have enough to deal with already. Maybe I was wrong."

"Talk to them," Nancy urged. "I'm sure you can work out an arrangement."

"I'll do that," Lena said with a nod. "Now, about this afternoon. I think it would be helpful if you organized a game of newcomb with some of the seventh-grade kids."

"What's that?" asked Bess.

"I know," Nancy said. "It's like volleyball, but not as rough. Instead of hitting the ball back over the net, you catch it and toss it back. Right?"

"Right," Lena said. "Everybody likes it. What do you say?"

Bess grinned. "Since Nan and I are both *newcomers*, I'd say leading a game of newcomb was made for us!"

"The seventh graders are down in the rec room, having an early snack," Lena said. "Josh should be there, too. He'll find you a ball and go with you to show you where the volleyball court is. Oh—and take paper cups and a jug of water with you. Playing newcomb makes the kids thirsty."

"Will do," Nancy said. She and Bess went down the two flights of stairs to the rec room.

Nancy was just about to open the door when she froze.

From the other side of the heavy wood door, she heard a gruff voice. "I don't care if you think it's wrong. We've got to teach them a lesson. Do as I say or you'll be sorry."

5

Unnecessary Roughness

Bess put her hand on Nancy's arm. "Nancy! Who—?" Bess whispered.

Nancy put her finger to her lips, but it was too late. A silence fell on the other side of the door. Clearly whoever had been talking had heard Bess's voice.

Nancy grabbed the knob and started to turn. At that instant, the door flew open and Maria came charging through. She rammed into Nancy and Bess, who stumbled backward, almost falling on top of each other.

"Watch it, you two," Maria growled. "You're in the way."

Bess glanced over at Nancy and gave her a look of disbelief.

Nancy darted past Maria and through the doorway. No one was close by. At the far end of the room, a crowd of noisy kids clustered near the snack table. Dino spotted Nancy and began walking toward her.

"Hi," he said. "When are you going to teach me judo?"

Nancy shook her head. "That wasn't judo. Just basic self-defense," she said. "Listen, Dino, did you notice anybody standing here by the door a minute ago?"

The boy thought for a moment. "Nope," he offered matter-of-factly. "I was busy trying to get some apple juice. I didn't get any, either. I wish people would line up, instead of just crowding around."

"Why don't you try again?" Nancy suggested, peering over his shoulder. "Looks to me like the kids are starting to move away from the table now."

"Good idea," Dino said. "See you." He darted away.

Nancy looked around. Bess was standing near the door, talking to Josh. Where had he come from? Could it have been his voice they had overheard? she wondered. The words had been so muffled. Nancy walked over and joined them.

". . . a gallon jug should do it," Josh was saying. "If you run out, there's a fountain not too far away, so you can refill the jug. Are you worried about getting dehydrated?"

Bess laughed. "Not for myself," she said. She patted her backpack. "I have a bottle of fruit juice in here. I was just asking because I don't want the kids to get too thirsty."

"Don't worry so much," Josh said. "You have to worry more about dehydration in the summer. Nobody's going to faint or anything on a breezy day like today."

"Great," Bess said emphatically. "Now I won't worry at all."

"If we're going to have time for a game, we'd better get moving," Nancy said. She raised her voice to call out to the kids in the rec room. "Everybody over here. We're going to the park to play newcomb."

There were scattered cheers, and the crowd began to flow in her direction.

Josh slipped away. A few moments later he returned with a volleyball under one arm and a big plastic jug of water in the other. "Ready?" he asked. "Let's roll."

Nancy took the water jug from him, and they both shepherded the kids up the stairs and outside. As they were crossing the street to the park, Nancy found herself remembering what it was like choosing up sides for a game. You never knew when, or *if,* you were going to be picked,

43

and someone always went through the agony of being selected last. She decided she would do it differently today.

When they reached the volleyball court, Nancy dropped the water jug on the grass near one of the poles and looked around. The net was sagging badly in the middle. She sent Bess to the other end, and the two of them tightened it. Part of the fun of volleyball, and newcomb, too, was the way the ball zinged off a nice, taut net.

"Okay," Nancy called. "Everybody line up. One long, straight line."

One of the taller boys came over and asked, "Can I be one of the captains? I'm a good picker."

"Not this time," Nancy said, trying to soften the refusal with a friendly smile. In a louder voice, she said, "Now, we're going to count off, starting with Bess and me. *One.*"

Bess, taken by surprise, hesitated, then said, "*Two.*"

The count continued down the line until it ended at fifteen.

"Right," Nancy said. "Odd numbers on this side of the net, even numbers on the other side."

"Don't we get to choose?" the tall boy asked with a frown.

"We just did," Nancy replied. "It's a really fair

way to choose up sides. Let's see. Our team has one more player, so you guys can serve first."

She tossed the ball over the net to Bess, who caught it with a relieved grin.

After some confusion, and a few protests from kids who usually played on the same team, all the players found positions. Nancy was in the back row on one side. On the other side, a small boy got ready to serve. Standing at the back line, he looked at the net and said, "I don't know if I can throw it over. It's so far."

"You get to run two steps before you throw," one of the other kids said.

The boy took two running steps and slung the ball. It cleared the net easily. The girl right in front of Nancy caught it and tossed it in the direction of the front row. Dino and a girl with a brown braid down her back went for it. They bumped into each other. The ball bounced off Dino's shoulder and rolled under the net.

"Hooray! Our point!" A cheer came from the other side.

"Okay, guys, listen up," Nancy said. "From now on, when you go for a catch, call it, so we have no more collisions."

The next serve went into the net. The players on Nancy's team each moved over one position, bringing the girl with the braid from the front row all the way to the back to serve.

"Come on, Irina," Dino called. "Throw it through their hands."

Irina flung the ball fast and low. It scraped past the net, zipped between two of the players on the other side, and hit the ground. Now the score was one-one. Irina aced her next two serves, too. On her next serve, though, she threw the ball so hard it landed out of bounds.

As the game continued, Nancy found it harder to concentrate. Part of her was back at the center, replaying the remark she and Bess had overheard. Who was supposed to do something wrong, to teach them a lesson? What lesson? And most important, who had given the orders?

"Hooray!" Bess exclaimed, as her team made a point. Her face was pink, and her hair had come loose from her barrette. "Way to go, guys!"

Nancy smiled at Bess's enthusiasm and tried to get more involved herself. The kids seemed to be having a good time.

On game point, the ball crossed the net over a dozen times. Finally it grazed the top and fell back on Nancy's side. Dino dived for it. All he got for his effort was a grass stain on his jeans.

"Good game, everybody!" Nancy called out.

"Let's play another," someone shouted. There was a chorus of "Yeah, let's!"

Nancy checked her watch. She wasn't sure if there was time for a game. Just as she was about to suggest a brief volley instead, someone announced, "This time, I'll play."

Nancy looked around. Maria was standing next to the court. She had a challenging look on her face. Half a dozen slightly older kids were with her. The only one of them that Nancy recognized was Brittany.

"We're doing okay," Nancy said.

"The way to learn a game is to play with someone who is better than you," Maria said. "I'll play on the team opposite you. They're missing a player anyway. That's fair."

Nancy felt a strong urge to tell Maria they were doing fine without her. It didn't seem wise to say anything to Maria in front of kids she'd been working with for so long. In any case, Nancy concluded, counselors weren't supposed to argue or disagree in front of the kids. It was bad for morale.

Maria took up an end position at the net and proceeded to tell the rest of her teammates where to stand, including Bess. No one seemed surprised at being ordered around by Maria. Nancy sensed that some of the spirit had drained from the players' faces.

"We'll serve," Nancy announced, tossing the ball to a boy named Patrick. He threw it toward the middle of the other court. Maria ran over, caught it before the player in that position had a chance to get near it, and jumped up to spike it over the net.

"Our serve," she called smugly.

Every time the ball crossed to her side of the net, Maria either caught it or ordered whoever did catch it to pass to her. Then she hurled it over the net with so much force that the players on Nancy's team started trying to keep out of the way of the ball instead of trying to catch it.

Before long, the score stood at seventeen-four. The boy who was serving for Maria's team sent the ball in Nancy's direction. She caught it and tossed it to Dino, who was front and center. He faked left, then threw it over the net to the right corner. A girl in a red shirt barely managed to catch it.

"To me," Maria directed her teammate.

The girl passed the ball to Maria. Maria turned, jumped up, and flung the ball over the net with all her might, straight at Dino.

Dino didn't have time to get ready or even to get out of the way. The ball hit him in the stomach. He doubled over and fell to the ground, clutching his middle with both hands. Nancy and Bess rushed over to him.

"I'm okay," he said faintly. There were tears in his eyes, but he blinked them away angrily.

"You're sitting out the rest of the game, Dino," Nancy told him as she helped him to his feet.

"Don't worry. The way it's been going, you won't miss anything."

As Nancy and Bess helped Dino to the sidelines, Maria yelled, "Come on, play ball!"

Nancy spun around. "We've got an injured player," she said. "Just hold on while we take care of him. And please don't go anywhere after the game. I want to talk to you."

For one moment, a look of anger crossed Maria's face. Then she lifted her chin and narrowed her eyes, as if defying Nancy or anyone else to criticize her.

The remaining points passed very quickly. When the game was over, Maria tried to lead her team in a victory cheer. Hardly anyone responded.

Bess walked over to the sideline and started pouring cups of water for the players. Nancy went up to Maria, who eyed her warily.

"I'd like to make a suggestion," Nancy said in a low voice. "Newcomb isn't Olympic volleyball. The kids are supposed to have fun. Why not take it a little easier next time and make a point of getting everyone involved?"

"We won, didn't we?" Maria demanded.

"Uh-uh," Nancy said, shaking her head. "*You* won. The kids on your team mostly stood around and watched you act like a big star. And the kids on my team weren't playing newcomb at all. They were playing dodgeball. Take my word for it, it wasn't much fun."

"You think you can just waltz in and tell me what to do," Maria said. "Well, you're wrong. I've been part of CARING for years. I belong here, and you don't. If you don't like the way I handle the kids, tough. Just pack up and go back where you came from. Believe me, nobody will miss you *or* your snobby friends."

Nancy took a deep breath. But before she could figure out how to answer Maria's attack, she heard a strangled cry from behind her. She whirled around.

Bess was stumbling to her feet. Her face was bright red, her mouth wide-open. In one hand she held her bottle of fruit drink. With the other, she was clutching her throat.

6

The Heat Is On

Nancy dashed over to Bess to help her.

"Water!" Bess gasped. "Please. Water!"

Nancy rushed over to the water jug. Dino was already there. He poured a cupful and held it out to her, hands shaking. Nancy hurried back, placed it in Bess's hand and watched helplessly as her friend brought the paper cup to her lips. Tear tracks gleamed on her cheeks.

"Bess, what is it?" Nancy cried. "Can you tell me what's wrong?"

Bess held up her bottle of juice, tears still streaming down her cheeks.

Nancy took the glass bottle, held it to her nose, and took a cautious sniff. It smelled citrusy, but with a funny edge to it, she thought. Nancy put the bottle to her mouth and allowed a few drops onto her tongue.

"Yuk!" she exclaimed. The tip of her tongue felt as if it were on fire. Tears rushed to her eyes.

Someone had dosed Bess's drink with four-alarm hot pepper sauce.

Nancy took a quick look around. Most of the faces showed only curiosity and concern. But one was carefully blank. It was Maria's. Was she responsible for playing such a dirty trick on Bess? Nancy wondered. She was tempted to accuse her on the spot, but held herself back. What evidence did she have? Nothing more than a fleeting expression that she might be misinterpreting.

Dino came over with the water jug. "Are you okay?" he asked Bess. "You want more water?"

Bess silently held out her paper cup for Dino to fill. She promptly drained it once more.

"What happened?" Dino asked. "Did something go down the wrong way? Why don't you hold your hands up over your head? That works for me sometimes."

"It was something in my drink," Bess managed to say at last. "Something that burned my mouth."

Wide-eyed, Dino exclaimed, "Really? Wow! You ought to sue the company. You'll make a fortune!"

"It wasn't the company's fault," Bess said. "I had a few sips earlier. It was okay then."

"You didn't happen to notice anybody near Bess's backpack, did you?" Nancy asked.

Dino's eyes grew wider still. "You don't mean somebody tried to poison her, do you?"

"No, no," Nancy said. "It wasn't poison, and it could have been an accident. But I'd still like to know how it happened. That's all."

Nancy glanced around. The kids had gradually lost interest in the drama of Bess's sickness. They were starting to wander away. Nancy called, "Hey, everybody, over here. We're heading back to the center."

Nobody listened.

"Time for cookies," Nancy added. This time, the kids circled around.

Back at the center, Nancy and Bess sent the kids down to the rec room with one of the other counselors, and then went looking for George. They started up the stairs just as George was on her way down. Seeing the distressed expressions on their faces, George took the steps two at a time. "What's the matter? Is anything wrong?" she asked.

"Let's go sit outside," Nancy replied.

They found a bench in one corner of the yard,

half-hidden by rosebushes, and sat down. Bess told George about her spiked fruit drink. Nancy followed with her suspicions of Maria.

"Wait, Nancy," Bess said. "That's not possible. Remember? Maria showed up with some of the older kids and started playing right away. She was on the court every minute until the end of the game. I went over to take a drink right after the game ended. There wasn't any time for her to mess with the bottle."

Nancy replayed the afternoon in her mind. Bess was right. Maria couldn't have doctored the fruit drink.

"Then who could have done it?" George asked.

"Well—" Bess and Nancy said in the same breath.

"Go ahead, Nan. You first," Bess said.

"Anybody watching the game from the sidelines," Nancy said. "And when we rotated positions and changed servers, some of the kids went over to take a drink. The water was right next to Bess's pack."

"But Maria *didn't* leave the court, even for a drink," Bess added. "I'm positive of that."

"It sounds like Maria's the one person who's definitely not responsible," George said.

"I wouldn't say that," Nancy replied.

"But, Nan—" Bess protested.

"I know, I know. She couldn't have put the hot sauce in herself," Nancy said. "But what if she told someone else to do it?"

"That conversation we overheard," Bess exclaimed. "Of course!"

Seeing George's puzzlement, Nancy explained, describing in detail the way Maria had suddenly barged through the door.

"So you think she was telling someone to dose Bess's drink," George said. "Who? Any idea?"

Nancy shrugged. "Maybe one of the older kids who were hanging around her. They were all sitting within easy reach of Bess's backpack."

"Hold on," Bess said with a frown. "I think we must be on a wrong track. How could Maria know I had that drink with me?"

"We've been through that. She saw you drink from it between games," Nancy said.

"But that conversation we overheard took place half an hour earlier than that," Bess pointed out. "Are you saying that Maria's accomplice was carrying around a bottle of hot sauce just in case?"

Nancy looked up at the sky thoughtfully. Bess was right—her scenario was a little extreme. Yet she was sure there was an element of truth to it.

"I just have a feeling Maria was going to watch

us until she got her shot," Nancy said. "When she saw your bottle of fruit drink, she signaled her accomplice to go ahead."

Bess nodded. "It's possible, I guess. Two things we know for sure—that hot sauce wasn't in there earlier, and it didn't get into my drink by itself. Look, Nancy, there's Dino. He looks like he's looking for someone."

Nancy glanced around. As she did, Dino spotted her, waved, and came running over.

"I solved it," he announced breathlessly. "I know who put the hot sauce in Bess's drink. It was Brittany."

Startled, Nancy looked over at Bess. Brittany had been sitting on the sidelines, near Bess's pack, during the game of newcomb. And now Nancy recalled seeing her in the rec room after the mysterious overheard conversation.

"Why do you say that, Dino?" asked George.

Looking at Bess, he said, "Your backpack is dark blue, right? Well, I asked around, and I found a kid who saw Brittany unzipping it while we were playing newcomb."

"Who saw this?" Nancy asked. "Was he or she sure?"

"It was Irina," Dino replied. "She's sure she saw Brittany opening a dark blue pack. *And* she says she had some kind of bottle in her hand. Now what do you think?"

"I'd like to speak to Irina myself," Nancy said.

"Irina's waiting for us inside," Dino said. "And Brittany's down in the basement, playing Ping-Pong. I saw her just a few minutes ago."

Nancy, George, and Bess stood up and started toward the front door. Dino trailed a few steps behind, looking both eager and a little afraid.

Irina stood nervously against the back wall of the lobby area, but quickly confirmed what Dino had said. Nancy tried to get more details from her, but Irina could not provide them. "All I know is that Brittany had a bottle in her hand and unzipped a blue pack."

"Okay, thanks, Irina," Nancy said. To Bess and George, she added, "Let's see what Brittany has to say about this."

They reached the rec room just as Brittany was handing over her paddle to another player and leaving the Ping-Pong table.

Nancy approached Brittany. "Can I talk to you for a minute?" Nancy asked.

"Why? What's the matter?" Brittany asked.

"Do you know what happened to Bess this afternoon, after the newcomb game?" asked Nancy.

"I heard there was something yucky in her drink," Brittany replied.

"Do you know anything more about it than that?" Nancy asked.

"No, why should I?" Brittany said. "Hey, what is this?"

Nancy took a deep breath. "Somebody thought they saw you unzipping Bess's backpack. This person said you were holding a bottle. Brittany, did you put hot sauce in Bess's fruit drink?"

"You're crazy!" Brittany declared angrily. "I wouldn't do that!"

Nancy glanced over at her friends. Was Brittany telling the truth? she wondered. "Somebody saw you," Nancy repeated.

Hands on hips, Brittany turned to face Bess. "What does your pack look like?" she demanded.

"It's dark blue," Bess replied.

Brittany spun on her heel and stomped over to the side of the room. A moment later she returned. She had a dark blue backpack over one arm. She unzipped it and pulled out a plastic bottle of spring water. "Is this what you're looking for?"

Nancy could feel her cheeks growing warm.

"I know why you're picking on me," Brittany continued. "It's because of what happened yesterday, isn't it? It was an accident. Didn't I say I was sorry? Just wait until I tell Lena about this!"

"Brittany," Nancy said, "we clearly made a mistake, and you're right to be angry. We apologize. But you can understand why we thought—"

"I don't care what you thought or why. Just leave me alone!" Brittany turned and rushed away.

After a short silence, Nancy said, "Well, we messed up that time, didn't we?"

Neither George nor Bess had any comment.

Dino came over and eagerly asked, "What did she say?"

Nancy replied, "Brittany's backpack is blue, too, Dino. And she had a bottle of water in it. That must be what Irina saw."

Dino's face went blank. Then in a low voice, he said, "Oh. I guess I goofed. Sorry." He walked away before Nancy could say any more.

"If this keeps up, I'm sure not going to win any popularity contests around here," Nancy said. She sighed. "All right, what next?"

As if in response, Josh appeared in the doorway and hurried over. "Lena wants to see us all in her office, right away," he said.

"What's up?" George asked.

Josh shook his head. "I don't know, but she sounds really upset."

The office was already full of volunteers when Nancy and her friends arrived. They crowded into a corner and waited. Nancy couldn't believe that Brittany had already complained to Lena about her.

A few moments later, Lena hurried in. "I'll make this quick," she said, after shutting the door. "We sent out four teams of sellers this afternoon. They struck out completely. Not one single sale. You know why? Because teams from YES covered those exact areas yesterday, selling *their* energy bars."

"That's a pretty strange coincidence," someone in the back of the room said.

"Some coincidence!" Lena shot back. "YES covered those areas *knowing* we were planning to hit them today. And they couldn't have known unless someone from CARING told them. You see what that means, don't you?" Lena looked around the room.

"We've got a spy in our organization!"

7

Nancy on the Case

A moment of silence followed Lena's startling declaration. Then everybody in the room seemed to begin talking at once. Over the hubbub, Nancy heard Maria say, "What did you expect? That's what happens when you take in a bunch of outsiders who don't have any loyalty to the program."

Nancy sensed that several people were starting to glance at her, Bess, and George.

"Hold on, Maria," George called. "I resent that!"

"Go ahead, resent it," Maria replied. "You've done nothing but stir up trouble since you got here. Now you're trying to sabotage our fund-raising efforts. I wouldn't be surprised if you were sent here by YES in the first place."

Lena held up her hand for silence. "Look, let's not go around accusing people for no reason," she said. "We've got a serious problem here, and we have to put our heads together and get to the bottom of the situation."

"I have an idea," Josh said. "First of all, I want to say I've been around here longer than most of you, and I don't agree with what was just said about our newest volunteers. I think they're terrific. We're lucky to have them with us. And from what I see, the kids in the program agree with me."

Nancy heard what she hoped was a murmur of agreement from the crowd.

"Next," Josh continued, "one of our newest volunteers may be the answer to our problem. Nancy, isn't it true that you've solved a lot of mysteries?"

Nancy felt her cheeks grow warm. "Yes," she admitted.

"There you go, then," Josh said. "We need to find out if somebody really is leaking information to YES. And if so, who it is. It sounds to me like Nancy could really help us out. What do you think, Lena?"

Lena was silent for a moment. Then she

shrugged. "Why, sure, that's a fine idea, Josh. Nancy, are you willing to see if you can find out anything about this?"

"I'll be glad to do what I can," Nancy said. "I'll need everybody's help, though."

Kiara Baum, the soccer coach said, "You have our support, Nancy. We're all here to help the kids in any way we can."

"All right, then, that's settled," Lena said. "I'll make sure that you're all informed of any developments. Oh, and while I still have you here, don't forget to keep spreading the word about the in-line skating marathon on Saturday at the mall. It should raise a lot of money and be tons of fun, too."

People started to file out of the office. Quietly Nancy went over to Lena and asked, "Can you spare a minute? To get started on my investigation, I need some background information from you."

Lena glanced at her watch, hesitated, and then nodded. "Sure, Nancy. Stick around."

Nancy, Bess, and George waited while the office emptied. Lena closed the door behind the last counselor, and then turned to face the trio. "Do you guys work as a team?"

"Sometimes," Nancy replied. "That way we can cover more territory." She cleared her throat. Lena, she noticed, seemed to be upset by this information. Was it that she was doubtful about Nancy's ability to help? Or did she think that three people on the case would undermine Lena's authority? Nancy decided to put aside her thoughts about Lena for the moment and forge ahead with the investigation.

"Tell me," Nancy began, "how do you keep track of where you're sending sales teams? And how easy would it be for somebody else to get that information?"

Lena picked up a pencil and twirled it in her fingers. "Well, once we've done an area, I mark it on my wall map," she said. "Block by block. I also keep a list, detailing what sales were made. That way, I can figure out which neighborhoods we do best in."

Nancy went over to the map. "So all these blocks marked in red are the areas that CARING has already covered. Is that right?"

"Right," Lena replied. "No point wasting our time covering blocks more than once."

"What about people who aren't home when we go by the first time?" Bess asked. "I had a lot of those yesterday."

Lena shrugged and smiled. "We miss out," she said. "We can't do everything."

Nancy studied the map with a frown. "There's

something I don't understand," she said. "Your office is open a lot of the time. Anybody could wander in and look at this map. But if they did, all they'd find out is where we've been, not where we're going, right?"

"Right," Lena replied.

"So where is that information kept?" George asked.

"In my desk and in my head," Lena said. "Here, I'll show you."

She opened the center desk drawer, took out a spiral notebook, turned to a page, and handed the notebook to Nancy.

Nancy looked at the page and saw that the current date was written at the top. Underneath that were several lines of writing. Nancy read the first line out loud. "'Grove and Worth, from Putnam to Crowell.'"

"That means I assigned a team today to cover Grove and Worth Streets, between Putnam Avenue and Crowell Road," Lena said. "When they got there, they found out that YES had done those blocks just yesterday."

"How long ago did you plan the assignment?" Bess asked.

Lena smiled sadly. "That's the point, isn't it? I try to plan a week in advance. So I wrote this out last Friday."

"And anyone who knew that could have sneaked in and looked at the notebook," Nancy observed.

"I'm afraid so," Lena said. "Don't worry, from now on I'm going to write the plans in code and keep my desk locked. But that won't help us this week if the plans have already been stolen."

"Unless you change them," George pointed out.

A startled look crossed Lena's face. "Of course," she said. "Why didn't I think of that? I'll work out a whole new schedule this evening. I wonder how long it'll be before those guys across the park figure it out—if they ever do!"

"Hopefully they won't," Nancy said.

Lena laughed. "Right. Well, listen, do the best you can to figure out who's behind this. Thanks to my carelessness, practically anybody could have gotten in here and copied that information."

"We know it won't be easy," Nancy said. "But we've faced tough cases before. You can count on us to give it our best shot."

"Thanks," Lena said. "And I'm sorry I kept you so late."

"No problem," George said. "We'll see you tomorrow."

George accepted a ride home with Nancy and Bess. She climbed in back, then leaned forward between the two front seats to say, "I feel so bad that I talked you two into working with CARING. I thought it would be fun. Instead, you've had one hassle after another. You don't have to stick with it if you don't want to. I'll understand."

"George Fayne, you have to be kidding!" Nancy said. "Drop out when we have not one, but two mysteries to solve? Never! I know—you want us out of the way so you can unmask the bad guys yourself and get all the credit!"

"Besides," Bess said, "the kids are great. We really care about them. We're not giving up now."

"Good," George replied. "Okay, so now what?"

Nancy was silent while she made the turn across the traffic on Washington Avenue. Then she said, "Tonight, I'm going to try to dig up some background information on both organizations. And tomorrow I'd like to find time to visit YES and talk to some of the people there."

"Uh-oh," Bess said. "You'd better hope that dear, sweet Maria doesn't spot you going in there. She's already convinced that you're the great-granddaughter of Benedict Arnold, the biggest traitor of all time."

"You probably won't have time to go by there anyway," George said. "Tomorrow's the day we take the kids to the pool. It's a madhouse. By the end of the afternoon, I guarantee you won't have any energy left over for detective work."

At ten-thirty that evening, Nancy pushed her chair back from the computer and flipped through the notes she had taken. She had lists of the current board members of both CARING and YES. She had the names of some of the prominent figures in River Heights who had attended a benefit dinner for YES. Many of the same people were among those who had bought tickets to a circus performance to benefit CARING.

She also had the computer address of the state office where the annual reports of charitable organizations were kept on file. In theory, any member of the public could download the information at will.

Nancy tried to hold back a yawn. She didn't expect to find anything important in the two annual reports. She had the impression that YES and CARING were both worthwhile organizations that happened to be in strong competition with each other.

The question was, had that competitive spirit inspired somebody to do things that, if not criminal, were at least unethical? If so, he or she should be stopped and exposed. Otherwise, the good works of the two organizations might end up being undermined.

Nancy suppressed another yawn. She shut down the computer, then went upstairs and got ready for bed.

Moments after she turned out her light, the telephone rang. She groped for it in the darkness. "Hello?"

"Sweet dreams, Nancy," a muffled voice said.

Nancy sat up. "Who is this?" she demanded.

"A friend," the voice replied. "With some good advice. Whatever's going on with CARING and YES, it's none of your business. If you want to stay healthy, you'd better back off."

8

Off the Deep End

"The tone of the person's voice was so cold. I'll never forget it," Nancy said to Bess. It was the next afternoon, and Nancy stood at the edge of the municipal pool next to Bess.

Suddenly, she interrupted herself to call out, "Hey, slow down, please. No running."

"Just the idea of getting a crank call makes me shiver," Bess said in a low voice.

"The worst part is, the caller had to be somewhere nearby, watching my window. How else would the person have known when I turned out my light?"

"Oh, that is creepy," Bess said. "Do you have any idea who it might be?"

Nancy shook her head. "No, all I know is that it has to be someone who was at the meeting with Lena yesterday, or who heard about the meeting from someone who was there. And there's another thing. During the call, I heard music playing in the background, as if the caller was at a club or something."

Nancy broke off what she was saying to watch two boys in the pool who were starting a water fight. She was about to approach them when she saw George make a sleek racing dive into the pool and swim toward the boys. The situation was soon under control.

An abrupt movement to her left caught Nancy's eye. She turned to look just in time to see Brittany take a running start off the diving board, launch herself into the air, and tuck her body into a cannonball.

"Watch out!" Nancy shouted.

Her warning came too late. Brittany landed squarely on top of George. For a moment, Nancy's view was blocked by a spray of water. When it settled, both George and Brittany had vanished beneath the surface of the pool.

Alarmed shouts sounded from all sides of the swimming pool. Nancy called out to the lifeguard, then rushed to the edge of the pool and jumped in. Three powerful strokes brought her to the area where she had last seen George and Brittany. She jackknifed into a surface dive and peered anxiously through the water.

She spotted George and Brittany at once. They were below her, near the pool bottom. George was trying to get a lifesaving hold on Brittany, who looked stunned. Nancy swam down and grabbed Brittany's other arm, then motioned upward. George nodded. They kicked off together.

They broke the surface just as the lifeguard arrived. She quickly and efficiently took Brittany from them. George turned to float on her back. She was taking in deep gulps of air.

"Are you all right?" Nancy asked, treading water next to her.

"I've been better," George said. "My back hurts. But not too bad. What happened? Did Brittany land on me?"

Bess swam up to join them, in time to say, "She sure did!"

George stared at her. "You don't think she did it on purpose, do you?"

"Let's talk about it later, when we're out of the pool," Nancy suggested. She glanced meaningfully at the kids near them in the water. "I want to make sure Brittany's okay, too."

Nancy, George, and Bess swam to the edge of the pool and climbed out. Brittany was seated on a bench, with the lifeguard on one side of her and Maria on the other. Her face was fixed in a resentful pout. When she saw George, her expression changed to a mixture of fright and defiance.

"How are you feeling?" George asked her. "That was scary, wasn't it?"

Brittany seemed surprised by the sympathy in George's voice. "Uh-huh," she said. "And the pool water tastes awful! *Blech!* Um . . . did I hurt you?"

"Not too bad," George said evenly. "It could have been a lot worse. What if you'd landed on top of one of the younger kids? Someone who wasn't a good swimmer? Next time, be sure to look before you leap."

"I'm sorry," Brittany said.

"I think Brittany's learned her lesson," Maria said stiffly.

"Good," George replied. "Well, if you're okay, we'd better get back to the other kids. We're still on duty."

As they walked away, Nancy said to George, "I wonder if you were too nice to her."

George looked at her, surprised. "She's just a scared kid," she said. "Accidents happen."

"True," Nancy said. "But not everything that looks like an accident *is* one. I caught a glimpse of Brittany's face just before she jumped. She looked angry and determined."

"You really think she tried to hit me?" George asked. "She hurt herself more than me."

"I don't know if she meant to land *on* you," Nancy replied. "But I do suspect she intended to get in your way somehow."

Bess cut in. "I'll bet she's still mad because we accused her of putting the hot sauce in my fruit drink."

"I was thinking about that," Nancy said. "We did make a mistake by accusing Brittany. Still, *somebody* put it there." She paused, lost in thought. "Do either of you see Irina anywhere?"

Nancy, Bess, and George scanned the pool area. "There," George said after a moment. "Just climbing out by the diving board."

"I'll be back in a sec," Nancy said as she walked over to the girl, who was squeezing water out of her braid.

"Hi," Nancy said. "How's it going?"

"Okay," Irina said. Nancy thought she sounded guarded.

"About yesterday," Nancy said. "Can I ask you a few more questions?"

"I never said Brittany was messing with your friend's pack," Irina said quickly. "Just that I saw her open a blue pack. I don't know whose pack it was."

"That's okay," Nancy said. "I see Dino told you what Brittany said. What I'd like you to do is try to forget that. Forget what you said to Dino. Just tell me what you saw, as if it's the first time you ever told anybody. What made you notice?"

Irina screwed up her face as she looked away, deep in thought. "I'd just rotated to the front row," she said. "I didn't like that. I was afraid I'd get hit by the ball, you know? And then I looked over at the sidelines."

"Why?" Nancy asked. "Anything in particular?"

Irina shook her head. "I don't know—Brittany was stooping down, with her back to the court. I thought that was funny. Everybody else was watching the game. And I saw that she was putting something in her pack, or taking something out. A bottle."

"Did you get a good look at the bottle?" asked Nancy.

"Not really," Irina said. "But I could tell that's what it was, because of how the sun reflected off it and hit me in the face. Anyway, that's all. The next serve came, and I stopped looking at Brittany."

"Would you know that pack if you saw it again?" Nancy asked, without much hope. "Or the bottle?"

"No way," Irina said, shaking her head again. "I wasn't really looking. Sorry."

"That's okay," Nancy assured her. "You've been very helpful. Thanks."

"Sure," Irina replied as she started toward her friends.

Nancy turned to search for Bess and George, when she found her way blocked by Dino.

"I'm not giving up," he declared. "I'm not going to stop till I've questioned everybody who was at the game."

"Dino . . ." Nancy began, then stopped herself. The information Dino had given them the day before was a good lead. Irina had just reconfirmed it. The problem was that Nancy had let herself act on the information before looking at it from all angles. That wasn't Dino's fault, it was her own.

"All right, Dino," Nancy said. "But be sure to tell me anything you find out, even if it doesn't seem to make sense to you. Okay?"

A grin spread across Dino's face. "Okay!" he said. "And don't forget, you promised to teach me martial arts. We can start as soon as we crack this case. Tomorrow, maybe."

He strutted away. Nancy laughed. If Dino was being a nuisance, at least he was a cute nuisance.

After an hour at the pool, the kids changed out of their swimsuits and headed back to the center for snack time. Nancy set off in the opposite direction, across the park to the headquarters of YES.

The one-story concrete building had a flat roof and a horizontal line of windows. It didn't look very welcoming, Nancy thought with a shudder.

The man at the desk inside the front door was not very welcoming, either. Nancy had to sign in and show him her driver's license before he allowed her inside. He then directed her to an office down the hall.

The sign on the wall next to the open door read Kyle Handly, Assoc. Dir. Nancy tapped on the door frame and went in. A man of about twenty-five was standing by a file cabinet, leafing through some papers. He turned when Nancy entered the office.

"Hi. Didn't I see you at the soccer game a couple of days ago?" he asked.

"That's right," Nancy said. She introduced

herself. It seemed to her that his eyes widened slightly when he heard her name. Did he know about her? she wondered.

"I'm writing an article on how community organizations raise enough money to keep going," Nancy continued. "Lena Boling has been helpful, and I'm hoping you will be, too."

"Have a seat, Nancy," Kyle said. "What do you want to know?"

"CARING's door-to-door sales campaign seems to be a success," Nancy said. "I understand YES has started something similar. Is that right?"

"You know that 'Imitation is the sincerest form of flattery,'" Kyle said with a smile. "They did it. It worked. So we've been doing it, too."

Nancy nodded. "What about the danger that you'll get into conflicts over who goes where, for example? What if you both try to cover the same territory?"

"It could happen," Kyle said. "But we tell our teams if they find out that CARING has already been on a particular block, to move on to a different block. River Heights is a pretty big town. There's room for more than one fund drive."

"So in your opinion, this is an effective and problem-free way to raise money?" Nancy asked.

Kyle sat up straighter. "I didn't say that. In

fact, we're thinking about suspending the sales program, for a while at least."

Startled, Nancy asked, "Why?"

"You're probably not aware of this, but there's been a wave of burglaries in town lately," Kyle said. "People are getting nervous. They aren't as ready to open their doors to our kids as they used to be. Sales are starting to drop."

For the next ten or fifteen minutes, Nancy continued to ask Kyle questions about YES's funding operations. Finally, she felt she had learned as much as she was likely to on this visit. She thanked him and stood up to go.

"Thank you, Nancy," he replied with a smile. "Drop by again sometime. I'd like to hear about some of the mysteries you've solved."

Outside the building, Nancy shook her head ruefully. Kyle had known all along who she was. Did he also know that she was working as a volunteer at CARING? She wondered if she could trust anything he had told her.

On the other hand, why would he lie to her? she thought. As she started across the park, Nancy found herself wondering about Lena's idea that someone in CARING was spying for YES. Would it make any sense for Kyle to send his sales crews to areas where Lena had planned to send hers? As he had pointed out, River

Heights was big enough for both groups. Could there just be a giant coincidence at work here?

Nancy decided to head directly to Lena's office to discuss these issues, but just as she arrived, Maria ran down the hall.

"Lena, you've got to do something right away!" Maria blurted out, pushing past Nancy. "George Fayne is stealing money from the organization!"

9

To Catch a Thief

A wave of anger washed over Nancy. George was one of the most honest, upright people Nancy knew. How *dare* Maria accuse George of being a thief! Nancy thought indignantly.

Nancy took a deep breath. She put her hands in her pockets to hide the fact that they were trembling. Keeping her voice as level as she could, she said, "You'd better explain that accusation, Maria."

"You bet I'll explain it," Maria spit out. "Three days ago I gave George an envelope to give to Alex. I would have done it myself, but I had to leave early. Inside was all the money I'd collected for energy bars over the weekend. It came to more than three hundred dollars. Now Alex says he never got it."

"Now hold on, Maria," Lena said forcefully. "Those are serious accusations. Why don't we find out what George and Alex have to say about this, before we go any further."

"Alex is gone for the day," Maria said. "I happened to catch him on his way out. That's how I found out about this."

Lena picked up a copy of the daily schedule. "George should be downstairs coaching Ping-Pong," she said, reaching for the telephone.

Nancy, Lena, and Maria waited together in tense silence for George to appear. A couple of minutes later, George hurried in, breathless from running up two flights of stairs. "What's wrong?" she asked.

Maria started to speak but Lena held up a hand to stop her. She turned to George. "Do you remember getting an envelope from Maria to give to Alex?"

"A couple of days ago? Sure," George said.

"Did you give it to him?" Lena asked.

"Sure," George said. "That same afternoon."

Maria took an angry step toward George. "He says he never got it," she said. "And there was over three hundred dollars in there."

"I don't know what was in it," George said

calmly. "You'd sealed the flap. But I handed the envelope to Alex and told him it came from you. Whatever was inside when you gave it to me was still inside when I gave it to him."

Maria's face reddened. "Are you calling me a liar?" she demanded.

"No," George said. "I'm not. But what if I was? That's no worse than calling someone a thief, is it?"

George turned to Lena and added, "Why don't you ask Alex what happened to the envelope?"

"Don't worry, I will," Lena replied. "But he left for the day. And he told Maria he didn't get the envelope, so we still have a mystery on our hands. Um . . . Nancy? Do you think—?"

"You're not going to ask *her* to investigate, are you?" Maria cried, breaking in. "She and George are best friends!"

"We have to have confidence in our colleagues," Lena said. "If Nancy can't be impartial, she'll turn the investigation over to someone who can. Fair enough?"

"That's okay with me," Nancy said. She thought, but didn't say, that since she *knew* George wasn't a thief, her investigation on that front would be nonexistent.

"Well, it's not okay with me," Maria declared. "I'm going to carry out my own investigation and find out the truth. Maybe I'm not a famous detective, but at least I'm not buddy-buddy with the main suspect!"

Before anyone could reply, Maria rushed out of the room.

"She's not thinking clearly," Lena said apologetically. "She and her kids worked hard for that money."

"I can imagine," George said. "But that's no excuse for lashing out at other people."

"Don't worry, Lena," Nancy said. "We'll get back the money and find out what happened. Can you give me Alex's home number?"

"You can't call him at home," Lena said. "His number's not in service. Some kind of mix-up with the phone company. But he'll be in tomorrow, sometime after noon."

Nancy and George left Lena's office together. On the stairs, Nancy said in a low voice, "The other day, when Bess and I met Alex for the first time, he had just bought a big bunch of CDs. He spent over three hundred dollars on them. In cash."

"The same amount that's missing," George said. "That's a funny coincidence."

"A coincidence or something else," Nancy replied. "It's worth checking out."

They were just crossing the front lobby when Dino rushed up.

"I found a really important clue," he announced. "Wait till you hear."

"What is it, Dino?" Nancy asked cautiously.

He gave her a shrewd look. "I was thinking about what happened to Bess," he said. "And I thought, people don't just carry hot sauce around with them. So it had to come from somewhere. And where do you find hot sauce?"

"In a Mexican restaurant?" George said.

Dino scowled at her. "You're making fun of me," he said.

"No, we're not, Dino," Nancy said quickly. "Please go on."

"You find it in a kitchen, that's where," he said. "So I went downstairs and asked Alice, who runs the kitchen, if she keeps hot sauce around."

"And does she?" George asked.

Dino smiled triumphantly. "Uh-huh. But when she looked for it, *it wasn't there!* Somebody must have taken it."

"Way to go, Dino," Nancy said. "I'm impressed."

"But that's not all," he said. "I asked Alice, and the last time she used the hot sauce was on Tuesday—the day before it got in Bess's drink. And whenever she's not there, she locks up, to keep people from taking cookies and stuff."

"But in that case, how could anybody get in to steal the hot sauce?" George asked.

"With a key, of course," Dino replied. "And only two people with CARING have keys—Lena and Maria."

"And only Maria was at the newcomb game," Nancy said, almost to herself. "It holds together but it's all circumstantial. No one actually saw Maria taking the hot sauce or passing it to Brittany, and no one saw Brittany putting it in Bess's drink. We may think we know what happened, thanks to Dino's terrific detective work. But we can't prove it."

"Anyway, face it," George said. "A dumb practical joke isn't nearly as serious as what we're dealing with now."

"What's that?" Dino asked eagerly. "Another mystery?"

"Nothing we can talk about now, Dino. Maybe later," Nancy said.

"Oh. Well, okay," he said. "But promise you'll let me help?"

"If I can," Nancy replied.

That evening, a meeting kept Nancy's father late at the office. Nancy had dinner at the kitchen table with Hannah Gruen, the Drews' housekeeper. Hannah had taken care of Nancy ever since her mother had died when Nancy was three.

They had just finished their chicken pot pies

and were about to start on a favorite dessert Hannah called raspberry fool when they heard Carson Drew's car in the driveway. A few moments later, he came in through the back door.

"Hi, Dad," Nancy said. "Did you have dinner yet? There's another pot pie in the oven."

"That's a tempting offer," Carson replied. "But I had a sandwich at my desk earlier. I didn't have dessert, though."

Nancy brought another dessert plate and a fork to the table. While Hannah dished up the raspberry fool, Nancy asked, "What's new downtown, Dad?"

He smiled. "Nothing much. Oh, I was talking to a reporter friend this morning, and those burglaries came up. I remembered your interest, so I asked him to fax me a list of addresses of the houses that were robbed. Here it is."

Nancy took the list. There were about fifteen addresses on it, arranged by date.

"All of these had three things in common," Mr. Drew continued. "They're all in well-to-do neighborhoods, the houses all have alarm systems that the burglars managed to circumvent, and the burglaries were all during daylight hours."

"Thanks, Dad," Nancy said. She tucked the paper in her pocket. "I'll see if I can come up with some ideas."

*　*　*

The next day, Nancy drove to CARING early, before the kids arrived. Lena was in her office with Alex. When Lena saw Nancy at the door, she beckoned her in.

"Good news," she said. "Tell her, Alex."

"That money?" Alex said, looking shamefaced. "It's not missing. I had it all along."

"Really?" Nancy said. "But didn't you tell Maria—"

"I know, I know," Alex said, breaking in. "Look, here's how it was. When George gave me that envelope, I didn't look in it, I just stuck it in my desk drawer. Then I got a long phone call. By the time I got off, I didn't even remember the envelope. So when Maria asked me if I got the money, I didn't know what she was talking about."

"Maria thought George had stolen it," Nancy said. "It really got ugly."

"I know." Alex sighed. "And I'm sorry. But at least the money isn't really lost. See?" He took an envelope from his jacket pocket and pulled out some crisp twenty-dollar bills.

"You'd better get that into the bank, before you put it down somewhere and forget it again," Lena said.

Nancy saw Alex flinch at Lena's cutting tone. "I'm on my way right now," he said. "Sorry for the mix-up."

He took a portable CD player from his backpack, put on the earphones, and pressed the Play button. Nancy heard a faint classic jazz tune. Alex gave them a jaunty wave and left.

"That's one mystery solved," Nancy said, smiling. "I wish they were all that easy."

"What about the spy from YES? Do you think you're getting anywhere?" Lena asked.

"I don't know. I'm not even sure there *is* a spy," Nancy replied. "And I do want to talk to you about that, but I want to take care of a few other things first. I'll be back."

Nancy went downstairs to see if Bess or George had arrived. She was eager to tell them that the money had not been missing after all.

She was nearing the alcove that held the pay phone when she heard someone say, "Nancy Drew is too smart. She's bound to figure it out."

It was Josh's voice, Nancy was sure of it. Nancy stopped to listen.

"Look, Kyle, I'm sorry," Josh said. "I know I agreed. But it's just too risky. We can't keep it up. Any minute now, this whole thing could blow up in our faces."

10

'Blading to Danger

Josh, a spy for YES? Nancy could hardly believe it. She liked him and respected his obvious concern for the kids in the program. How could someone like that also be deliberately trying to undermine the program?

There was a click as the phone was replaced in its cradle. Before Nancy could move, Josh stepped out of the alcove. The shocked expression on his face told Nancy what she needed to know.

"Uh . . . Hi, Nancy. Did you—?" Josh stammered.

"I heard you mention my name, if that's what you want to know," Nancy said. She looked evenly at Josh, not sure whether to think of him as a friend or an enemy.

"I knew it'd come out sooner or later," Josh said, looking nervously down the hallway. "With your detective skills, you must have started to suspect."

"No, I had no idea," Nancy admitted. "I was even starting to wonder if Lena was imagining things. Then to find out that there really is a spy from YES, and that it's you—"

"Spy! Hey, wait a minute," Josh protested. "I'm no spy. Where'd you get that idea?"

"You were just talking to Kyle Handly," Nancy said. "You told him what you've been doing is getting too risky. Don't tell me you were busy arranging a Frisbee tournament."

Josh stared at her. "That's amazing! As a matter of fact, a Frisbee tournament *is* one of the ideas we've been tossing around."

"I was being sarcastic," Nancy said. "Come off it, Josh. What exactly have you been doing for Kyle and the others at YES? Passing on information about where CARING's sales teams are scheduled to go? That's what Lena thinks."

"Hold on, you've got the wrong idea," Josh started to say.

"Or is something bigger at stake?" Nancy asked. "Selling a few more energy bars wouldn't mean much one way or the other. But what if you're giving YES inside information about

Lena's fund-raising plans—that could be worth real money to them."

"You're crazy!" Josh exclaimed, glaring at her. "You spend so much of your time hunting for crooks, you're starting to see them everywhere!"

Nancy squared her shoulders. "But that still doesn't explain what you said on the phone to one of the chief honchos at YES—that something is getting too risky."

Josh sighed heavily and said, "Okay, look. Here is the whole thing. This rivalry between CARING and YES is getting out of hand. Some of our kids and some of theirs almost got into a fight on the street yesterday. We're supposed to be community organizations, not gangs!"

"That's true," Nancy said. "Kyle was out of hand at the last game, too! He's not setting a very good example."

"Sometimes he gets carried away." Josh shook his head. "He and I agree the way to cool down the hostilities is to work together," Josh said. "We've known each other since we were little. It was our idea to cosponsor the skating marathon at the mall this weekend. We were hoping we could follow it up with other joint programs."

"Is that what you were afraid I would figure out?" Nancy asked. "I'm sure it's not a huge secret."

Josh hesitated and glanced around, as if nervous that they might be overheard. Lowering his voice, he said, "The fact is, when I talked to Lena about more cooperation with YES, she wasn't interested. At all. So I decided to go ahead on my own. She finally okayed the skating marathon, because we'd already lined up sponsors. She could see that it was going to be a success. But if she found out Kyle and I had even bigger plans . . ."

Nancy narrowed her eyes. She was positive there was something more here, something Josh wasn't telling her. Why was Josh so nervous about being discovered? Unless he really *was* acting as a spy.

"Josh," Nancy said. "Was Lena right? Have you been giving Kyle information about where the CARING sales teams are about to go?"

His face turned pale. With pleading in his eyes, he said, "It wasn't like that! You've got to understand. We got nervous that if kids from the two groups ran into each other while they were selling door-to-door, they'd get into a fight. Sure, I told Kyle where our kids were going. But that was so that he could make sure the kids from YES *didn't* go there."

"But instead, they went there a day earlier," Nancy said. "Isn't that what really happened?"

93

"I don't understand it!" Josh blurted. "Kyle's baffled, too. The only thing I can think of is that Lena changed the schedule at the last minute and sent them to places she hadn't written down."

"And just happened to send CARING teams to the neighborhood where YES had been the day before?" Nancy said skeptically.

"Yes. It could have happened. It could have just been a coincidence," Josh said. "I can't help it. You can see why I didn't want you or anybody to find out. We weren't doing anything wrong. But I realize how bad it looks. You believe me, though, don't you?"

"I hear what you're saying," Nancy said. "And I think I just might believe you."

Josh did not look satisfied by her answer. Before he could continue, however, George and Bess walked in the front door and cheerfully approached them.

"Hi, Nancy. Hi, Josh," Bess said enthusiastically. "How are you?"

"Fine," Josh muttered. "I have to run, though. See you later." Without looking at Nancy, he headed for the stairs, which he took two at a time.

Bess watched him go, her face a mixture of puzzlement and hurt. She looked over at Nancy.

94

"He was in an awfully big hurry to get away from us," she said. "Is anything wrong?"

"Let's go sit outside," Nancy replied. "There's a lot I have to catch you up on."

The three friends returned to the benches in the rose garden. Nancy told George and Bess about Alex finding the missing money, then about Josh's phone call to YES, and his explanation of it.

"Do you believe him?" George asked.

"Sort of," Nancy said. "What he told me fits a lot better with the kind of guy I thought he was than one who's actually out to wreck CARING. I know it leaves a lot of questions unanswered, but I'm willing to trust him at this point."

"Let's see what we have so far," Bess said. "The missing money isn't missing, so that question is answered. The YES spy may or may not be a spy. That question is *not* answered. The question of who put the hot pepper sauce in my fruit drink is still up for grabs. . . ."

"We can make a good argument that Maria put Brittany up to it, but I'd like to find some proof. If they think they got away with it, they may pull more stunts like that. And I don't have to tell you who their targets will be. They've made it pretty clear they'd like us out of here."

"As you say, we need proof," Bess said. "We thought we had a witness. Then it turned out that

Brittany could explain what Irina saw. She wasn't putting hot sauce in my drink, she says. She was getting a bottle of spring water from her own pack."

George glanced at her watch. "We've got a few minutes before most of the kids get here," she said. "Why don't we reenact the events? Maybe we'll notice something we didn't see before."

"Good idea, George," Nancy said. "But I don't think we have time right now. Don't forget, we're scheduled to take a bunch of kids over to River Heights Park to practice their skating. We want our guys to be prepared for the skate-a-thon."

"Hey, that's right," Bess said. "Okay, how's this? Why don't we plan to get here a little early tomorrow. I'll bring a bottle of fruit drink *and* a bottle of hot sauce. Do either of you have a dark blue pack?"

"I do, somewhere," Nancy said. "I'll be sure to bring a bottle of spring water, too."

George stood up. "All right, that's set," she said. "I'd better run and say a word to Lena before we head for the park. I'm glad that money turned up. I was starting to wonder if maybe I was to blame."

"That Maria is dangerous," Bess said. "I hope when she finds out the truth, she feels ashamed of herself for accusing George."

"Let's be fair," Nancy said. "The money *was* missing, and Maria *had* given it to George. Her accusation wasn't completely unreasonable."

Bess laughed. "Oh, Nancy, you're impossible," she said. "Why do we always have to be so fair and reasonable? Can't we enjoy being a tiny bit *un*fair now and then?"

Nancy grinned. "Well . . . maybe just among ourselves. As long as we know that we're doing it. Come on, it's skating time."

A group of kids had already gathered near the front door when Nancy, George, and Bess walked around to the front door of the center. While George counted heads, Nancy went inside to get her yellow-and-black in-line skates. They were on the floor of the hall, next to her backpack.

"Hi," Dino said, as Nancy picked up her gear. "I'm ready to help you with your new case. What's it about?"

"Case?" Nancy said. "Oh, sorry, Dino. It turns out there wasn't any mystery after all."

He gave her a suspicious look. "You're just trying to keep me out of it, aren't you?" he said, sounding hurt and angry. "You think I'm too young to be any help."

"That's not—" Nancy started to say. But Dino stomped away without listening.

97

I'll have to talk to him later, Nancy thought as she went outside. But what would she say? She didn't want Dino to feel left out, but she also didn't want his enthusiasm to get in the way of the investigation—or to get him into trouble or danger.

Nancy sat on the front steps and put on her safety pads and skates. Then she, Bess, and George checked the safety gear of all the kids.

George skated over to Nancy. "I'll lead, Bess can take the center, and you bring up the rear," she suggested. "The only tricky part will be crossing streets. Once we get to the park, we can relax and have fun."

River Heights Park was about a dozen blocks away. The streets they had to cross were not busy, and the kids behaved themselves on the trip.

Once in the park, George led the group down a long sloping path that ended at a wide promenade overlooking the river that ran through the town and gave it its name.

As Nancy approached the riverbank, she looked back to make sure that no skaters were lagging behind. She lifted the front of her right skate off the pavement, hoping to engage the heel brake so she could slow down.

Suddenly Nancy felt a jolt, as if she had skated

over a big bump. But the pavement was smooth. She looked down and gasped in horror.

The rubber brake pad had come off Nancy's skate. The pavement dipped sharply, and Nancy could do nothing to slow herself as she careened wildly toward the riverbank.

11

On the Brink of Disaster

Nancy flew helplessly down the hill toward the river. Ahead, only a low railing separated her from the water. It was worse than no block at all, Nancy thought frantically. If she ran into it, Nancy knew she would flip over and hit the river headfirst.

For an instant, Nancy thought of throwing herself to the ground. That would certainly stop her, but at what cost? She was wearing strong, plastic knee, elbow, and wrist guards in addition to her helmet, but they were meant to break falls on level ground, not on hills.

Nancy looked around frantically and realized that her only hope was to try to get herself over to a patch of grass near the railing.

Calling on her training and agility, Nancy shifted her weight entirely to her right skate. She turned her left foot sideways and pressed the sides of the wheels against the concrete in a maneuver she knew was called the Power Slide.

There was a loud, scraping noise. Helped by the decrease in slope of the walk, she began to slow down. Immediately she got into a crouched position and turned left, heading for the grass. When she reached the grass, she stopped short and fell sideways. Her safety gear and the soft grass softened the fall, and Nancy barely felt the impact. She lay on her side, not knowing whether to laugh or cry.

"Nancy! What happened?" George asked, skating over to her.

"Are you all right?" Bess called out.

Nancy took a deep breath and willed her racing pulse to slow down.

"I lost my brake," she said. She bent over and flipped the release levers on the skate, then slipped her foot out. Picking up the skate, she took a careful look at the metal bracket that was supposed to hold the brake pad in place.

It was as she remembered. Normally, the rubber pad was held in place by a quarter-inch steel bolt that passed all the way through the pad and screwed into the bracket on the other side. Now, the bolt was gone, along with the brake pad, but the bracket was undamaged.

No, Nancy thought. This was no ordinary mechanical failure. The bolt must have been unscrewed but left in place, set to fail the first time she really needed the brake. She looked closer and saw a few thin scratches around the bolt hole, probably left by a screwdriver.

"I never heard of somebody's brake pad breaking off," George said.

"Neither have I," Nancy said grimly.

George opened her mouth. Then, noticing the ring of curious kids that had formed around them, she shut it again. It was clear she had understood what Nancy had implied.

Nancy put her skate back on. "Too bad I don't play roller hockey," she said, trying to sound cheerful and carefree. "In-line hockey skates don't have brakes in the first place. Bess, will you set up the slalom cones? Okay, who wants to make the first run?"

Back at the center, Nancy and her friends sent the kids down to the rec room for snacks. This was the first moment they had had to talk privately since the terrifying incident with Nancy's missing brake.

"Are you sure it couldn't have been an accident?" Bess asked, half worried, half hopeful.

"Absolutely sure?" Nancy repeated. "Brake pads don't just fall out. I would have noticed if that bolt had been loose. Plus, I don't see how it could work itself loose."

"Nancy, I don't like this at all," George said. "Putting that hot sauce in Bess's drink wasn't funny. Still, you can see how someone with a warped sense of humor might think it was a joke. But this isn't funny. It was only quick thinking on your part that kept you from being badly injured."

"I know," Nancy said. "I don't like it either. We've got to find whoever's doing this before something serious does happen."

"Your skates were sitting in the hall for, what, half an hour?" Bess asked. "Longer? Anybody could have tampered with them."

"Yes, but people go back and forth all the time," Nancy pointed out. "Somebody may have noticed something. Let's fan out and ask." She sighed. "People are going to get awfully tired of all this interviewing. . . ."

They went downstairs to the rec room. The noise level was staggering. It sounded as if every kid in the room was talking at once. Nancy looked around, trying to sort out where to begin.

Somebody tugged at her sleeve. It was Dino. He cupped his hands to his mouth and stood on tiptoe to approach her ear.

"I heard what happened to you," he said loudly. "I know who did it."

Surprised, Nancy gave him a doubtful look. He nodded vigorously. Nancy pointed to the door and followed him out of the room.

"I know who did it," Dino repeated, once they were in the stairwell. "I saw her."

"Who did you see?" Nancy asked. "And what?"

"When I got here this afternoon, Brittany was sitting on the floor in the hall," Dino said. "She had a screwdriver in her hand, and she was fiddling with a skate."

"Are you sure, Dino?" Nancy asked.

"Of course I am," he replied. "I didn't think anything about it then. But when a kid told me about what happened to you, I put two and two together." He grinned.

Nancy sighed. "It's just hard to believe Brittany would risk a trick right now, especially since she was suspected of putting hot sauce in Bess's fruit drink."

"Ask her," Dino said. Then he added, "Can I come with you?"

"No," Nancy said gently. "We have to think of Brittany's feelings. I'll let you know what happens, though."

Nancy returned to the rec room and found Brittany sitting at a table, taking a sip from a plastic bottle of spring water. Her expression hardened, Nancy noticed, when she saw Nancy approach her.

"Go away," she said as soon as Nancy was close enough to hear her. "Leave me alone."

Nancy pulled out a metal folding chair and sat down. "Brittany, I need your help," she began. "I need everyone's help. Somebody tried to sabotage my skate today."

"Oh?" Brittany said in a bored voice. "Too bad they didn't do a better job."

Nancy felt anger rise in her. Instead, she said, "It's not funny. I could have been badly hurt. Brittany, when you were in the hallway earlier, did you see anybody with my skate?"

"You think it's me again," Brittany declared. Her voice trembled, and her eyes shifted from side to side, as if she wanted to bolt and run from the rec room.

"No, I don't think it's you, Brittany," Nancy continued calmly. "Somebody saw you using a screwdriver on a skate, and I have to follow every lead."

"You're crazy!" Brittany said. "I didn't touch your skates. Maybe somebody saw me working on mine. Upstairs in the hall, around three-thirty?"

"Your skate had a problem, too?" Nancy asked.

"I just got them," Brittany said. "They have an active braking system, and I had to adjust it."

She reached under the table and pulled out a pair of in-line skates. They were purple and black, Nancy noticed—the new kind with a lever down the back of the right skate that activated the brake.

"I did use a screwdriver," Brittany said. "So maybe that's what your tattletale saw."

"Okay, Brittany, thanks," Nancy said. "I believe you. But I still need help in catching the culprit. Please come and tell me if you saw anything suspicious."

Nancy put a reassuring hand on Brittany's shoulder. Then she stood up and walked across the rec room. After a moment, Dino caught up to her.

"Those skates you saw Brittany fiddling with, were they yellow and black?" Nancy asked Dino.

Dino shook his head. "Nope. Purple and black. What happened? Did I just goof up again, Nancy?"

"Don't worry about it, Dino. Detective work is full of false leads and dead ends. You have to learn to observe very carefully and not jump to conclusions. And keep going in spite of disappointments. Okay?"

By the time Nancy left to go home, she had to remind herself of what she had told Dino earlier. In comparing notes on the skating accident, she and George and Bess realized that none of them had found anything they could call a solid clue. No one had noticed anyone doing anything to Nancy's skate.

Hannah was sitting at the kitchen table leafing through a magazine when Nancy walked in. She looked up with a welcoming smile. "There's fresh lemonade in the refrigerator."

"Thanks, Hannah." Nancy poured a glass and sat down. In the center of the table was a plate half-full of very familiar-looking crunchy bars. Nancy took one and munched on it.

"Good, aren't they?" Hannah said. "My visitor this afternoon said they were the best she'd ever tasted."

"Visitor?" Nancy asked. "Who was that?"

"A nice girl who came to the front door selling healthy snacks," Hannah said. "She said it was to benefit an after-school program for children. She left a few samples."

Nancy laughed out loud. "Hannah, I'll bet that's the program *I'm* working with, along with Bess and George!" she said. "Was she wearing a green T-shirt?"

"Why, yes, she was," Hannah said thoughtfully.

"What was the girl's name?" Nancy continued. "I must know her."

Hannah shook her head. "I'm afraid I didn't

catch her name. But she had long blond hair, and she was wearing glasses with heavy black frames."

Nancy frowned. She couldn't think of anyone from CARING who looked like that. Who could it be? she wondered. And come to think of it, what was she doing around here anyway? The schedule Lena had shown her for this week didn't bring CARING sales teams anywhere close to the neighborhood where the Drews lived.

On a hunch, Nancy reached for the telephone and dialed the CARING office. Lena was still in.

Nancy gave her address and asked, "Were any of our kids near here this afternoon, selling energy bars?"

"No," Lena said. "This afternoon, everyone was totally wrapped up in getting ready for the skate marathon on Saturday. We didn't send out any sales teams at all."

12

The Phantom Seller

Nancy replaced the receiver. If the girl who had come to the house that afternoon *wasn't* a CARING volunteer, then who was she? Nancy wondered. And what was she up to?

"Hannah," Nancy said thoughtfully, "tell me more about this girl."

"Was there something wrong with her?" Hannah asked.

"I don't know," Nancy admitted. "It's possible. How was she dressed?"

Hannah tossed her head. "Like you. Blue jeans and a T-shirt. Green, like I said."

"Did the T-shirt say anything on it?" Nancy probed.

"I think so," Hannah said. "Nancy, what's wrong? Why all the questions?"

"Whoever this girl is, I don't think she really comes from my organization," Nancy explained. "But she's pretending that she does. I want to know why. These energy snacks she was selling—do you remember what she said about them?"

Hannah frowned in concentration. "No, I'm sorry, I have to confess I wasn't listening very carefully. I remember that the bars were high in all the essential vitamins and so on. Oh, and that they came in several flavors. I ordered a box of the cocoa flavor."

"You did order some, then," Nancy said. "Did you pay her for them?"

"Oh, no," Hannah replied. "I offered to, but she said I shouldn't pay until I received the energy bars. She even warned me not to be so ready to hand over money to strangers. We had a nice laugh together about that."

"I'll bet you did," Nancy muttered. Every instinct told her that there was something wrong with the visitor. But if she was running some sort of con game, it seemed to be a subtle one.

Could this visit simply be a way of getting to know Hannah and softening her up? Maybe the girl would return later with news of an investment opportunity guaranteed to triple Hannah's life savings. Or with valuable papers she had pretended to find, for which the owner was bound to offer a huge reward . . .

Dozens of clever, unscrupulous schemes were used every day to cheat trusting people, Nancy thought. All of these schemes depended on the charm of the person using it. And from what Hannah had said, the girl who had sat in the Drews' kitchen and eaten high-energy bars that afternoon was as charming as they came.

"Hannah," Nancy said, "will you let me know right away if you hear from this girl again? And if she mentions any kind of financial scheme, tell me or my dad about it right away. Okay?"

Hannah closed her magazine. "Nancy, please. I wasn't born yesterday. I'm not going to buy a gold mine from a stranger, or even a genuine Swiss watch at an unbelievable price. Like anyone else, I can be fooled. But only once, not twice."

Nancy went over and gave Hannah a hug. "I'll vouch for that," she said with a smile. "I remember once when I was little, I wanted to stay home from school because I hadn't finished my homework. I told you I was sick. You didn't believe me for a minute."

Hannah laughed. "For a minute, maybe, but no

longer than that," she said. "Was this the time you rubbed the thermometer on your blanket? You rubbed too hard. It read one hundred and six degrees. But when I put my hand on your forehead, it was cool."

Nancy grinned. "I should have rubbed my forehead on the blanket, too. I'll remember that next time."

Nancy picked up the phone and dialed George's house. "Can you think of anybody around CARING with long blond hair and black framed glasses?" Nancy asked when George answered.

"No. Why?" George replied.

Nancy related Hannah's story. "Something tells me this may be important," she concluded.

"I'll make some calls," George offered. "Maybe she's someone who used to be connected with CARING. I'll get back to you as soon as I know something."

Next Nancy called Bess. "I don't think I know anybody at CARING that you don't know," Bess said, concern mounting in her voice.

"Don't worry, Bess," Nancy said. "I'll let you know if I uncover anything. And don't forget about our reenactment tomorrow."

"I won't forget," Bess promised. "As long as you don't expect me to drink from the bottle after you've put the hot sauce in it."

"I don't expect us to be *that* realistic," Nancy promised.

Nancy pressed the Disconnect button on the receiver, then dialed another number. Over the next half hour, she spoke to five more CARING volunteers. None recognized her description of Hannah's visitor. Three of them suggested that the girl must be an imposter from YES.

"Bet on it," one volunteer told her. "This has to be some sneaky plot to make CARING look bad. What if they pass out rotten energy bars, pretending that they come from us? I wouldn't put it past them."

"I couldn't believe it," Nancy told George later. "Do they really think that the people in YES would go around deceiving the public, just to discredit a rival organization?"

"It seems incredible," George replied. "I got the same kind of comments as you did. A lot of our people have talked themselves into believing that YES is out to get us. And the only way they can think of to prevent it is to get them first. The level of hostility is pretty scary."

"We'd better be well prepared on Saturday," Nancy said. "We don't want the skating marathon to turn into the Rumble at the Mall!"

The next day was bright and sunny and Nancy once again picked up Bess and George early.

They left the car on the park side of the street, a block down from the Clelland Center, and walked to the volleyball court.

"The backpacks were on this side, near the pole," Nancy said. She put the blue backpack she was carrying on the ground. Bess put hers down next to it. George added a third, this one red.

"Now what?" George asked.

"Why don't you be Brittany," Nancy suggested. "And Bess can be Irina. I'll play any other parts we need. So, Bess, you're here, on the forward corner. George, you squat down with your back mostly to the court. Okay, action!"

"What do I do?" George asked plaintively.

"And me, what do I do?" Bess added.

"Let's see," Nancy said. "Why don't we run through it twice, with different scenarios? George, the first time you reach in your pack, take out the plastic bottle of spring water, take a drink, and put it back."

"And me?" Bess repeated.

Nancy shrugged. "You watch her do it. Ready . . . go!"

George unzipped the pack and groped around for the bottle of water. Finding it, she pulled it from the pack, unscrewed the cap, took a sip, replaced the cap, and put the bottle back.

"Cut!" Nancy said.

"Can I straighten up?" George asked. "My knees hurt."

"Sure," Nancy said. "As soon as you're ready, we'll try it the other way."

George shook out her legs. Then she squatted again. Taking the bottle of hot sauce from her pack, she undid Bess's pack, took out the fruit drink, removed the cap, and doused the bottle with sauce. It seemed like only moments before Bess's pack was closed again, the hot sauce was out of sight, and George was getting to her feet.

Nancy wrinkled her forehead. "The second version didn't really take any longer than the first," she said. "So now we know that someone might have tampered with Bess's drink without anyone noticing. But I can't help feeling we're missing an important clue."

Nancy looked around the court, then up at the trees and the sky. There was something that Irina had said, something that didn't fit with one of the versions she had just watched.

"George, stoop down again and hold the water bottle to your lips," Nancy said.

George did as she was told.

"Now take out Bess's bottle and hold that up so that it's just above the opening to the pack," Nancy continued.

Looking puzzled, George followed Nancy's orders.

"That's it!" Nancy exclaimed.

"It is?" Bess said. "What?"

"Irina said the bottle Brittany was holding glittered in the sunlight," Nancy explained. "But her spring water bottle is made of plastic. It doesn't glitter. Bess's fruit drink comes in a glass bottle, though, and it *does* glitter. So what Irina saw Brittany holding was the fruit drink bottle, *not* the bottle of spring water."

"The hot sauce bottle is glass, too," George pointed out.

"It doesn't matter," Nancy insisted. "Whether she was holding the hot sauce or Bess's drink, either way Brittany is our culprit. And personally I can hardly wait to tell her—and Maria—what I know and how I know it."

They gathered up the packs and started toward the center. As they crossed the street, they saw Josh coming down the sidewalk. He waved as he called George's name.

"I'll find out what he wants and meet you inside," George said to Nancy.

"I'll stay with you," Bess said to George.

Nancy shrugged, then turned to go inside. Bess still seemed to have a strong interest in hanging around Josh, no matter what he was up to.

The entrance hall was empty as Nancy passed through it on her way to the rec room. As she neared the door to the steps, she heard a familiar

116

voice. It was Brittany talking. Nancy moved forward quietly and listened.

". . . put up with them any longer," Brittany was saying. "Now listen up. I'll tell you how we can get even with those creeps from YES."

Nancy held her breath. She didn't want to miss a word. Suddenly, she heard the faint sound of a shoe brushing against the tiles. It came from behind her. She started to turn. At that moment, an arm snaked around her neck.

Nancy gasped. The arm tightened on her throat, choking Nancy and causing her to gasp for air.

13

Stranglehold!

Nancy reached up with both hands and grasped her attacker's forearm. As she pulled it away, she turned her head so that the front of her throat could rest in the crook of her attacker's elbow. If necessary, she knew she could use several karate moves that could free her, but only at the risk of seriously injuring her attacker. Nancy saw that as a last resort.

Nancy searched for a sensitive spot on the forearm and pressed her fingertips into it. The tension in the arm loosened a little. Nancy caught a quick breath, then shouted, "Let me go!"

She heard running footsteps. Josh yelled, "Maria, stop it! Are you crazy?"

The pressure on Nancy's throat eased. She spun around and taking a step backward faced Maria. The girl's face was twisted into an angry expression. George and Bess were there, holding her by the elbows.

Lena came running down the stairs. She pushed through the crowd of kids that had gathered in the hall. "What on earth is going on here?" she demanded, looking from Nancy to Maria.

"Maria just jumped Nancy from behind and tried to strangle her," George reported.

Nancy rubbed her throat and didn't say anything. She wanted to hear how Maria would explain her attack.

"I just caught her snooping again," Maria practically hissed. She jerked her arms away from George and Bess, who did not argue, but remained by her side.

"She was trying to listen in on some of the kids without their knowing," Maria continued. "All I wanted to do was protect their privacy. I don't think we should allow a bunch of sneaks to come in, take over our program and act as if they belong in everyone's business. They should all be thrown out, right now."

Dino pushed his way to Nancy's side. "I don't think we should have counselors who go around starting fights," he said, scowling at Maria.

"You just wait, Dino," Brittany growled. "I'll fix you."

"You just try it," Dino retorted.

"Nancy, what's this all about?" Lena asked.

"I *was* trying to listen when Maria grabbed me," Nancy said.

"See?" Maria crowed. "What did I say?"

"There was a reason," Nancy continued, raising her voice. "I overheard Brittany talking to some other kids about getting even with people from YES. I think that's a terrible idea, so I listened to find out what Brittany was planning."

"That's a lie!" Maria shouted. "You and your buddies are still trying to frame her and me. Just yesterday you tried to say that she sabotaged your skates. Even your own so-called witness changed his tune, didn't he?"

"I did not accuse Brittany of anything," Nancy replied calmly. "But now I'm sure that Brittany put hot sauce in Bess's fruit drink. Someone stole the hot sauce from the kitchen, and you have a key. And a witness saw Brittany dosing Bess's drink with it during the newcomb game."

"I already told you that all I did was take a drink of water from the bottle in my own pack," Brittany said, her voice rising.

"I'm sorry, that's not true," Nancy retorted. "Your water was in a plastic bottle. But our

120

witness saw a bright reflection of the sun off the bottle you were holding. The sun would only reflect off a bottle made of glass, not plastic. Both the fruit drink and the hot sauce were in glass bottles. Come on, Brittany, tell the truth!''

Brittany stared at Nancy. Her cheeks were pale. She shifted her gaze to Maria. Suddenly her face crumpled. She covered it with her hands and began to sob.

Maria rushed over and put her arm around the girl's shoulders. "All right, it's true," she said, keeping her eyes fixed on Lena. For the first time Nancy heard a softer tone in Maria's voice. "We did doctor Bess's drink with hot sauce. But don't try to blame Brittany. The whole thing was my idea. It was just a joke, a way of welcoming Bess and Nancy to the program."

"A way of chasing us away, you mean," Nancy said.

"What about sabotaging Nancy's skates?" Bess asked. "Was that your idea of a joke, too?"

Maria scowled at her. "We didn't touch Nancy's skates," she declared loudly. "I don't care if you believe me or not, it's the truth. I would not place someone else in that kind of danger. Ever. I'll bet her skates were simply defective."

"I don't think this is getting us anywhere. Let's

121

break it up," Lena said. "Josh, you've got a volleyball game now, right? Nancy, Bess, how are you at Frisbee?"

"Pretty good," Nancy said, not taking her eyes off Maria.

"Okay," Lena said. "Take the twelve-year-olds over to the meadow in the park for an hour. And, George, I'd like you to coach another group on soccer passing."

"But I'm supposed to do that this afternoon," Maria said in surprise.

Lena nodded. "I know," she said. "But I need to talk to you. In my office."

"Oh, no, you don't," Maria replied, setting her jaw. "Whatever you've got to say to me, you can say it right here, in front of everybody."

Lena's face colored. "All right, Maria, if that's the way you want it. You've been part of CARING a long time. Longer than any of us. And we all know how much you want to make the program a success. But lately you've changed. You've done your best to drive away our new volunteers. If this keeps up, we're going to have to take a long, hard look at your future participation."

Maria's eyes narrowed. She took a deep breath. For a moment, Nancy was sure that she was going to blast Lena. Then her shoulders fell. She let out a breath slowly. "I understand," she said in a low voice.

"Good," Lena said. "We'll say no more about it, then."

Suddenly, Nancy felt sorry for Maria. Sure, Maria had asked for it, Nancy thought. Still, to be humiliated in front of the kids couldn't be easy.

Nancy noticed that Lena seemed uncomfortable, too. She looked around at the circle of spectators and raised her voice to say, "Okay, kids, let's get moving. We're wasting the afternoon."

Nancy and Bess gathered their group together and led them across the street to the park. Dino walked beside Nancy. "Didn't I tell you? I knew it was Brittany who doctored Bess's drink!" he said, brimming with excitement.

"Yes, you did tell me, Dino," Nancy said. "And you're the one who found Irina and got the testimony that proved it. I think you're going to make a very good detective one day."

Dino beamed. "Now I want to help you solve the skate mystery," he said. "I really thought I had the answer. But all I ended up doing was showing that Brittany *didn't* do it."

"Knowing who isn't guilty can be a big step toward figuring out who is," Nancy told him. "That's called the process of elimination."

"I'll remember that," Dino said solemnly.

The Frisbee game was livelier than Nancy had expected. By the end of the hour, she and Bess were ready to quit, while the kids looked ready to play for another hour. Only the lure of snack time persuaded them to stop playing and return to the center.

As they crossed the street, Nancy saw Alex drive up in a blue van and park, a cell phone to his ear, and a jazz tune playing loudly on the van's stereo. He caught sight of Nancy and waved.

George's group was already in the rec room when Nancy, Bess, and their group arrived. Nancy and Bess made sure that their kids got cookies and juice. Then they grabbed cups of juice themselves and joined George at a table in a relatively quiet corner of the room.

"So what do you think, Nancy?" George began. "Who did the dirty work on your skates? Maria and Brittany denied it. Do you believe them?"

Nancy ran a hand slowly through her hair and let all the facts about the case tumble through her mind. "I'm tempted to," she said finally. "Maria seemed genuinely upset at the idea that I might have been injured. And remember Dino's testimony—when Brittany was working on her own skates, mine were nowhere in sight."

"So what do you think happened?" Bess asked.

"Well, let me think about it. If someone were

going to sabotage my skates, would he or she do it right out in the open, where somebody might see?"

"The way Dino remembered seeing Brittany adjusting her skates," George said. "So you think the bad guy picked up your skates, went somewhere to loosen that bolt, and brought them back? But that means whoever did the job had to have someplace private to do it. Otherwise, it would look even more suspicious than doing it in the hallway."

"Good point, George," she said. "And wherever it is, it's probably close to the hall. You wouldn't want to hike very far with somebody else's skates in your hand."

Alex appeared in the doorway. Raising his voice, he said, "Can I have your attention?"

Silence fell slowly, helped along by a chorus of shushing.

Once the room was quiet, Alex continued. "Counselors, we're going to have a short meeting about energy bar sales. Lena's office, right away. And everybody, don't forget the skating marathon tomorrow. A bus will leave the center at nine-thirty sharp, or you can meet the rest of us at the mall."

Nancy, George, and Bess threw away their paper cups, then started up the stairs. Maria was a little ahead of them, walking slowly. She glanced over her shoulder and seemed about to say something to them. Then she apparently changed her mind. She began to take the stairs more briskly.

Lena's office gradually filled up. Nancy recognized all the counselors by sight. She still had five or six names to learn. She looked around to see if anyone matched the description of the person who had sold Hannah the energy bars. No one matched the description even remotely.

Lena rapped her knuckles on her desktop and said, "I'll keep this brief. It's Friday afternoon, and I know you want to get home. Plus we have a very event-packed day tomorrow. But I'd like to ask you to share your recent experiences going door-to-door. What seems to work? What are the problems? How can we make the sales program more productive? Anyone? Yes, Stella?"

A young woman with short hair framing a round face said, "I've tried sending the kids up to houses singly and in pairs. I have the feeling we get about fifty percent higher sales with pairs. Does that fit with anybody else's experience?"

Josh raised his hand and said, "Yes and no. We get higher sales, but it takes twice as many kid-hours to make them. So it pretty much comes to the same thing."

That got a few laughs. A young man with dark hair falling over his forehead said, "Josh may be right, but the kids like it better when they go in pairs. It's less scary for them."

"Has anybody else been questioned by the police?" Nancy asked. "I was stopped the other day."

There was a flurry of yeses. "The cops pretty much know us by now," Stella said. "But when we go to a new neighborhood, it's a problem."

"What if we tell the police ahead of time where we're going?" someone asked.

"That idea's been raised already," Lena said, with a glance in Nancy's direction. "I'm looking into it. I don't think it's quite as easy to do as one might think. . . ." She glanced at her watch. "Oops—sorry, I have to run. I'm meeting a potential donor. I'll see you all tomorrow at the mall. And don't forget to bring all your friends. We'll have a great time."

The meeting broke up slowly, as everyone stood around, eager to share sales stories.

Finally, Nancy, Bess, and George left the building and got into Nancy's car.

"I hope Maria isn't too upset about being scolded in public," Nancy commented as they moved away from the curb. "She really does care about the program and the kids."

"She asked for it," George pointed out. "The worst part, if you ask me, was her bringing Brittany into her plan."

"Unless it was the other way around, and Brittany got Maria involved," Bess said. "Anyway, Maria seems okay. I heard her kidding around just now with some of the other counselors. She said when she delivers the energy bars, she ends up with a wad of money so thick that it stretches the pocket of her jeans."

"She makes that many sales?" asked George.

"No. It's that people always pay her in small bills." Bess laughed.

Nancy was preoccupied with edging past a double-parked car. It was another moment before she realized what Bess had said. She pulled over to the curb and stopped.

"What is it, Nancy?" Bess asked. "Is something wrong?"

"I'm afraid so," Nancy replied. "If Maria usually gets paid in small bills, what about the money she said George had stolen? Alex showed it to me. It was a stack of new, crisp twenty-dollar bills!"

14

Mayhem at the Mall

"I hope Alex is going to be here," Nancy said as she pulled into a parking spot at the mall. "I really want to ask him about that money."

"Why didn't you call him last night?" George asked.

"According to Lena, his phone isn't working," Nancy told her. "You'd think he'd get it fixed already."

"Too bad we don't have his cell phone number," Bess said. "Even if his home phone is disconnected, that one's working. We all saw him using it yesterday. So, Nan, you think Alex took that money to buy CDs?"

"Then replaced it when it looked like he might be caught," George said, completing the thought.

"That's the way it fits together," Nancy said. "Of course, he may say that he simply meant to borrow it for a day or two."

George looked grim. "There's a word for 'borrowing' money from an organization without proper authorization," she said. "Even if it's just for a day or two. And especially if you're the treasurer. It's called embezzlement."

Inside the mall, Josh rushed over when he saw Nancy, Bess, and George enter. "Just the people I need!" he exclaimed. "Will you give me a hand?"

Nancy noticed Maria walking by. "I'll catch up with you," she told Josh. Nancy moved past Josh to intercept Maria. "Hi. Can we talk for a minute?" she asked. "I want to straighten things out between us because I need your help."

"Is that so?" Maria responded warily.

"Look, Maria," Nancy said. "I'm not out to get you. I'm not trying to take over at CARING, and I'm not trying to pin something on you. George asked if I'd give some time to the kids in the program, and I agreed.

"It was a bad idea putting that stuff in Bess's drink and you know it," Nancy continued. "I had to figure out who did it. Then when that money seemed to be missing, Lena asked me to look into it. I agreed again, because I thought it was for the

130

good of the program. I think you want what's best for CARING, too. Can't we work together?"

"I don't know," Maria said. "You and your friends are changing the place. Why can't everything stay the way it was when I was younger? I felt totally at home then. Now, I'm not sure where I belong."

"You belong at CARING," Nancy assured her. "George, Bess, and I are there for the same reasons you are. We want to have a good time, and we want to help the kids. You do, too, don't you?"

"Well, sure," Maria said. "But it's not the way it used to be."

"Things change," Nancy told her. "And we have to change with them."

"I guess so," Maria said reluctantly. "But that doesn't mean I have to like it. Listen, what do you want, anyway?"

"I want to talk about that envelope you gave George to pass on to Alex," Nancy began.

Maria stiffened. "That again?" she said. "Didn't I say I was sorry? And it's not my fault if Alex stuck it somewhere and forgot about it."

"I'm not talking about blame," Nancy said. "Yesterday you made a joke about always getting stuck with a thick wad of small bills. What about

131

the money in the envelope? Was that in small bills?"

"Was it ever!" Maria replied, rolling her eyes. "And I'm not just talking about fives and tens. There must have been fifty dollars in singles! I had to recount it a couple of times to make sure the amount was right. Why?"

"I'm still trying to sort things out," Nancy said. She thought it would be better not to share her suspicions just yet. "Thanks for giving me a chance to talk to you," she added, giving Maria a warm smile.

"See you later," Maria said, the hint of a smile on her lips. "Have fun," she added tentatively as she hurried off.

Nancy's relief at Maria's softer tone was quickly replaced by the thought that she had to find Alex. She scanned the crowd but saw no sign of him. She did see Lena and hurried over.

"Alex?" Lena said. "No, I don't think he's planning to come. You can catch him on Monday if you need to. What's up?"

"Nothing that can't wait," Nancy said, trying to make her tone sound casual.

From someplace down the mall came a chant of "Go, go, go!" Nancy moved toward the enthusiastic cheers to see what was happening. Some moments later she found herself in the center of the mall's main gallery, where teams from YES and CARING were enjoying a shortened but heated game of roller hockey. The score was tied at one-to-one.

One of the CARING guards blocked a YES offensive and stole the puck, shooting it down the court to the forwards. But before the forwards could push through their march on the goal, the YES defense had made their own steal and sent the puck back down toward the CARING goal.

Three things struck Nancy about the game. One was the speed with which the play zipped from one end to the other and back again. The second was how often the players lost their balance and fell. And the third was how cheerful they seemed when they got back up onto their skates. Rivalry or no rivalry, they were obviously having fun.

Nancy divided her attention between the game and the spectators. When two kids near her started an argument about the strengths of their respective teams, she moved in quickly, before the verbal battle had time to get physical.

Nancy thought it was a shame that the organizers had structured so many of the events as competitions between CARING and YES. The kids would probably have enjoyed it just as much, and maybe more, if each team had people from both programs.

Nancy was also keeping an eye out for Alex.

As the hockey game ended in a draw, Bess joined Nancy. "What's next?" she asked.

"A team of trick skaters," Nancy replied. "Have you seen George?"

"She's helping a couple of other counselors ride herd on the older group," Bess said.

Nancy noticed a familiar face and waved. As the young man made his way over toward them, Bess said, "Hmm—who's he?"

"Kyle Handly," Nancy told her. "He's the big honcho over at YES. He's the one Josh knows really well."

"Hi, Nancy," Kyle said. He gave Bess a friendly nod. "I hear you were suspecting me of all kinds of sinister designs."

Embarrassed, Nancy shrugged. "Well, I hope you can understand . . ." she began.

"Of course," Kyle said good-naturedly. "Given this stupid rivalry, it's only natural. When we planned today's event, we actually hoped it would bring the two groups of kids together. Now I'll be glad if nothing happens to drive them further apart."

Kyle looked around. "I've got to get back to my kids. See you later," he said as he briskly walked away.

"He seems nice," Bess remarked.

"He does," Nancy said, letting her voice trail off. She wanted to believe he was nice, but she wasn't going to discount the possibility of his playing a role in the door-to-door sales problem.

The trick skating began, with the help of an array of brightly painted barrels, boards, and ramps. The more daring the stunt, the more the kids loved it.

Nancy watched for a bit, then walked over to help the people who were laying out the course for the junior slalom.

When the junior slalom started, Nancy, Bess, and George watched together. The young skaters were so cute and so determined that the spectators cheered for them all, whether they wore green CARING T-shirts or yellow YES T-shirts.

One of the competitors was Dino. He gave Nancy a thumbs-up sign before he made his run. His time put him in the middle of the pack, but his grin said that he was happy with it, anyway.

During a break to realign the cones that had been knocked out of place, Josh walked over. "I was looking for you guys," he said. "Can you run an errand? It's nearly time for the marathon, and our kids are out of pledge forms. Would you scoot back to the center and bring some back?"

"Sure," Nancy said. "Where are they?"

"In Lena's desk somewhere." Josh handed her

a ring of keys. "Don't lose these, whatever you do. And please be as quick as you can. Every pledge we miss is money we don't raise."

The drive to the center didn't take long. Nancy parked in front, and she, Bess, and George walked quickly inside and upstairs to Lena's office.

One of the keys opened the door to Lena's office. Another unlocked the desk. Nancy rummaged through the stacks of papers in the drawers, but she didn't see anything that looked like pledge forms.

"Where could they be?" she wondered aloud.

"Try the supply cabinet," George suggested. "I'll look in the files, under P for 'Pledge.'"

Bess joined Nancy at the cabinet. Its deep shelves were stacked with boxes of stationery, envelopes, and other supplies. They opened each one in search of the forms.

"That's funny," Bess suddenly said. "Why would Lena keep a wig in the supply cabinet?"

Nancy looked over, as Bess lifted a wavy blond wig from a carton marked Discs. There was something else in the box, too—a pair of glasses with thick, clumsy black frames.

Nancy grabbed the glasses, held them up, and peered through them. "This is just plain glass," she announced.

"Why would anyone—" George started to say.

Then she broke off and said, "Oh, I get it. They must be part of a Halloween disguise. CARING always has this big party and—"

"I think this may be the answer," Nancy said grimly. She took a sheet of paper from the bottom of the box. On the paper was a list of addresses, with a date next to each one.

Nancy recognized the list. It was the list of houses that had recently been burglarized.

Nancy scanned the list. She remembered that the one her father had obtained for her had fifteen addresses on it. This one had sixteen.

Nancy let her eye drop to the bottom of the list. The last address was on her own block—and the date next to it was today's date!

15

Chase to the Finish

"That's it!" Nancy nearly shouted the words. She showed the list to Bess and George. "Lena is part of the burglary ring," she said. "She's been going to people's houses as a CARING volunteer, wearing a disguise, and choosing the targets for the thief. She's already been to my house and spoken with Hannah. And today they're planning to rob the Colemans, down the block from me."

"We've got to stop them!" George exclaimed.

"Of course we do," Nancy said. "But we've also got to make sure they *stay* stopped. We'd better put this stuff back exactly the way we found it. But first, I need a photocopy of this list, showing the entry for today."

The photocopier was on the table next to

Lena's desk. It seemed to take forever to warm up, Nancy thought as she drummed her fingers nervously on the table. Finally the green light appeared.

Nancy made the copy, pocketed it, and then replaced the original of the list in the carton. Bess added the glasses and wig, and they put the box back in the supply cabinet.

Nancy locked the office when they left. "Let's hope Lena doesn't have a spare set of keys," Nancy said softly. "If she doesn't, the evidence is safe!"

On the drive back to the mall, Nancy felt an extreme sense of urgency. She had to watch the speedometer carefully so that she would not exceed the speed limit.

The mall parking lot was crowded. Nancy pulled into the first empty space she saw, miles, it seemed, from the mall entrance.

"We should skate," George suggested. "We'll get there a lot faster."

"Great idea," Nancy said, reaching for the trunk release. She, George, and Bess quickly donned their in-line skates and protective pads. Soon they were racing across the pavement. Near the entrance, a guard frowned and took a step toward them, holding up one hand. It looked as if he was about to tell them they couldn't skate inside.

Then a sudden loud cheer caused the guard to glance over his shoulder. Just a few yards away, in the main gallery, was an unbroken line of skaters taking part in the marathon. He shrugged and let the girls past.

Nancy and her friends skated alongside the line but at a faster pace. The registration stand for the marathon was halfway down the gallery, near the central bank of escalators. Nancy spotted Lena from twenty yards away just as Lena looked in her direction. Nancy could see a look of alarm cross Lena's face as the woman whirled and pushed off on her skates.

"Go after her, George!" Nancy cried. "Don't give her time to warn anyone. Bess, call the police!"

George dropped into a speed skater's crouch and pushed off. Nancy managed to stay close behind her. But Lena had spotted a tiny gap in the thick line of marathoners and darted through it. The gap closed before George and Nancy could follow.

George merged with the line of skaters, then edged step-by-step through it. Nancy did the same. Soon they were in the clear again. But by now Lena had a lead of fifty yards or more. In a few moments, she would be out of sight, Nancy thought desperately.

Nancy called up a mental map of the mall. The

next turn to the left led to the cinema multiplex, she knew. But she remembered there was a gallery at the end of that turn that rejoined this gallery at the food court.

"George!" Nancy called breathlessly. "I'm turning off. We'll trap her."

George quickly nodded, then began to skate even faster.

Nancy dodged around a family with twins in a stroller, slowed for a group of teens who were window-shopping six across, and excused herself as she broke through the line waiting to see a popular action film.

At last she had a clear stretch ahead. Her arms and legs swung in a smooth, synchronized rhythm that ate up the yards. She wished she could enjoy the idea of skating through the mall and forget that this was serious business. But she couldn't, she thought grimly.

Then she saw the food court straight ahead and brought her mind back to the chase. Had Lena already passed here on her dash to the mall's exit and freedom? No, here she came, weaving through the clusters of customers.

"Hey, watch it!" somebody shouted angrily. Lena had brushed against him, sending the slice of pizza and cup of soda on his tray flying. Around him, others were backing away and

141

screaming. They weren't sure what was happening, but they could tell it was trouble.

Nancy slowed and angled to the right, winding among the crowded tables. Lena saw her coming. She made a lightning U-turn around one of the tables. But just then, George appeared, streaking right at her. Lena grabbed a woman with a bag of tacos, pushed her into George's path, then looked around frantically for an escape route.

Nancy slid to a halt next to her. She grasped Lena's wrist and pulled her arm behind her back in a hammerlock.

"It's over, Lena," Nancy panted. "You're not going anywhere."

Detective Brunnell checked the list of dates and addresses against a page in his notebook. "And you say you found this in Ms. Boling's office?" he asked, looking from Nancy to Bess to George.

They were sitting in a conference room in the mall office. Lena had been taken away in handcuffs after refusing to say a word. Outside, in the gallery, the marathon was still going on, undisturbed. It wasn't scheduled to end for another hour and a half.

"Yes, we found the list and a disguise in Lena's office," Nancy told the detective. He had arrived only minutes before, called from home after

Nancy told the uniformed officers about the link to the wave of burglaries. "We left everything where we found it."

"This last address," Brunnell said, looking at Nancy. "It's on your block? That's quite a coincidence."

"Not really," Nancy said. She quickly explained how Lena, in disguise, had cased the block. "I'm sure Hannah—our housekeeper—can ID her, if that will help," she added.

"Shouldn't we be doing something?" George asked. "The gang is planning to rob the Coleman house *today*."

"I've already ordered a stakeout of the premises," Brunnell said. "Though I have to tell you this is pretty flimsy evidence. Every news organization in town has the same list, except for that last address. If we come up empty-handed, I'm going to have a lot of explaining to do."

"Detective Brunnell," Nancy said. "Is it okay if we leave now? We've had a long, exhausting day, and I think we all want to go home."

Brunnell squeezed his lower lip between his thumb and forefinger. "Hmm . . . I can't stop you from returning to your own homes," he said. "And I trust you understand what could happen to this case if you get in the way?"

Nancy jumped to her feet. "Of course! We'll see you later."

The three girls hurried out to the car and drove north through town. When they reached Nancy's neighborhood, Nancy said, "We should all look straight ahead, as if there are no cops—or robbers—around."

Nancy pulled into her driveway and stopped next to the garage. They hurried in through the back door. Hannah, in her usual chair, looked up in surprise. Nancy gave her a quick summary of what was happening.

"So we're going up to my room," Nancy finished. "If we keep out of sight, we can watch from there."

"I'll bring you up a snack," Hannah said.

Upstairs, the window next to Nancy's desk had a view down the street toward the Coleman house. Nancy positioned herself beside the window and peeked out. Bess and George stood behind her.

"We're staking out the stakeout," George said with a chuckle.

After ten minutes, Bess gave a sigh and sat down at the desk. "This is boring. Tell me if anything happens," she said.

"It may not," Nancy said. "They could have some kind of signal that Lena is supposed to give—no signal, no robbery."

"What if nothing happens here, and Lena keeps her mouth shut?" asked George.

Nancy shook her head. "The authorities might decide that they don't have enough evidence to press charges. She could go free."

"Hold it," George said urgently. "A blue van just pulled into the Colemans' driveway."

Bess sprang up and joined Nancy and George at the window. They heard the van door slam. For several long minutes, nothing happened. Then, suddenly, a dark sedan came speeding up the block and jerked to a halt, blocking the driveway entrance. Two uniformed officers jumped out and ran toward the back of the house.

"Come on!" George shouted, heading for the door. Nancy and Bess were close behind her.

A police officer stopped them on the sidewalk. They stayed with a little group of neighbors until another car arrived with Detective Brunnell in the backseat. He waved them through the make-shift barricade.

"Thanks to you, we caught him red-handed," Brunnell told them as they walked up the driveway.

"He?" Bess whispered to Nancy. "Who?"

At that moment, two officers came out the back door. Walking between them, his wrists hand-cuffed, was Alex Houston.

"Are you the guy in charge?" he said, when he saw Brunnell. "I want to make a statement. I'm just a little fish. The one you really want, the one who dreamed up the whole thing, is Lena Boling. She picked all the targets and figured out how to get around the alarm systems. I was just following orders."

Alex seemed to notice Nancy and her companions for the first time. "You!" he said. "We were doing fine until you came along. You ruined everything!"

"No, *you* ruined everything. You stole money that was supposed to help the kids at CARING. How could you do that?"

"You wouldn't understand." Alex nearly spat the words. "Those fat cats on the board of directors have no idea what it's like to exist on nothing. She wanted to help CARING, so she brought me in to help her make ends meet."

"You make her sound like a real Robin Hood," Nancy remarked. "Taking from the rich and giving to the poor. Lena went around in disguise selling energy bars, didn't she? She cased the houses, then you robbed them." Nancy paused to think a moment. Suddenly she smiled. "But then YES started selling, too. That must have complicated your lives."

Alex gave her a dirty look. "You think you know it all, don't you?"

"Was it Lena's idea to send teams to blocks she knew YES had already covered?" Nancy probed.

"I think so. That way, if anyone started thinking there was a link between the sales teams and the burglaries, they'd have to suspect YES as much as CARING."

"You mean they were trying to frame the kids at YES and CARING for the robberies?" Bess asked. "That's unbelievable!"

"We weren't trying to frame anybody." Alex shook his head with disgust. "We were both hoping nobody made the connection. But just in case they did, we figured the more tangled the whole business was, the better for us. It really threw us when you guys started poking around. We had to do something to keep you off balance."

A thought hit Nancy. "Is that why you took my skates to your cubicle and loosened the screw that holds the brake pad?"

"Who says I did that?" Alex replied with a smirk.

"It had to be somebody with a private place to do the dirty work," George said. "Maria and Brittany were already on our case. You must have calculated that we'd blame them for anything else that happened."

"And we'd be too busy watching out for more dirty tricks to notice anything else," Bess added.

"And that's why you made that anonymous call to me the other night, too," Nancy said. "You called from your van, didn't you? I half-recognized the tune that was playing in the background." She hummed a couple of bars.

"Duke Ellington, 'Take the A-Train,'" Alex said instantly. "Talk about a classic! But that doesn't prove a thing. Millions of people own that recording."

"Was it on one of the CDs you bought with the three hundred dollars you stole?" Bess asked. "That must have been rough, having to replace the money once Maria started making a fuss about it."

"Not as rough as standing here, listening to you three," he retorted. To the officer on his right, he added, "Can we get out of here? My fan club is starting to bug me."

By the time Nancy, George, and Bess got back to the mall, the marathon was ending. Dino noticed them and skated over.

"Guess what, Nancy!" he said, with a big smile. "I skated over ten miles. And I had pledges for five dollars a mile. That's fifty dollars for CARING. Isn't that great?"

"It sure is," Nancy said, giving him a quick hug. "I'm really proud of you."

"And Brittany raised almost a hundred dollars," Dino continued.

"That's fantastic," Nancy said. "I'm proud of both of you."

"Look, there's Josh," Bess said. "I wonder if he knows yet."

Josh waved and joined them. "Isn't this wonderful?" he said, gesturing toward the crowd of skaters. "I was just talking to Kyle. Today has been such a success that we think it's time to move toward more joint activities between CARING and YES. We're going to draw up a plan and take it to the boards of the two organizations. Who knows? We might even merge one of these days."

"That sounds like a step in the right direction," George said. "Count me in your plans."

"Good," Josh said. "I wanted to tell Lena, but she doesn't seem to be around. I'm worried about how she'll react. She's so used to being in charge."

Nancy looked over at George and Bess. The three of them started to laugh.

"Don't worry about Lena, Josh," Nancy said. "Something tells me she's not going to be a problem."

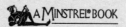

THE HARDY BOYS® SERIES By Franklin W. Dixon

LOOK FOR AN EXCITING NEW
HARDY BOYS MYSTERY COMING FROM
MINSTREL® BOOKS

DAUGHTERS *of* LIBERTY

<u>INDEPENDENCE DAY 1776</u>

It all started with the Daughters of Liberty
and their adventures in Philadelphia....

PATSY'S DISCOVERY

PATSY AND THE DECLARATION

BARBARA'S ESCAPE

By Elizabeth Massie

A MINSTREL BOOK

Published by Pocket Books

1337-02